STONE COLD BAD

STONE BROTHERS BOOK 1

NEW YORK TIMES BESTSELLING AUTHOR
TESS OLIVER
ANNA HART

Stone Cold Bad

2nd edition

Copyright © 2024 by Tess Oliver and Anna Hart

All rights reserved.

No part of this book may be reproduced in any form or by any electronic or mechanical means, including information storage and retrieval systems, without written permission from the author, except for the use of brief quotations in a book review.

ISBN: 9798884754362

Imprint: Independently published

ONE

JADE

"I will plunge this letter opener into your fucking eye!" I screamed.

Ray's hand clamped around my arm. My forearm looked like a brittle matchstick in his thick iron grasp. He squeezed hard enough that I was sure I could feel my bones squeaking against each other. The letter opener fell to the floor.

Ray's fingers were leaving a mark on my skin. I spit at him and waited for him to smack me. I'd never pushed him this far when he was drunk, but I'd been dragged to the limit. I just didn't care anymore. I wanted to be free of the bastard.

I squeezed my eyes shut and swallowed back the bitter taste in my throat. Ray's movements were clumsy, slowed by the alcohol. He spun me around, slammed my hands down on the desk and pounded my fingers once with his fist for good measure. I cried out in pain.

"Stand still, little bitch. Can't fuck a moving target when I'm this drunk."

I swallowed again to keep from puking my guts out all over his desk. Although it would have been fitting for the asshole. It hadn't always been this way, the bile, the tension in my jaw at the thought of having Ray's hands on me, but now all I could think was I wanted him dead. Sometimes, when he was grunting with exhaustion, pumping me, trying to get his whiskey soaked cock off, I would close my eyes and wish that his fucking heart would explode, right while he was inside of me, touching me, making me sick to my stomach. Then I would push his ugly dead carcass off of me, step right over him and walk out the fucking door for good. But no such luck.

"I told you I'm not in the mood," I tried one last plea. There had been a time when the man still had a thread of conscience, and he would have listened. But that man was gone, replaced by a greed driven, alcoholic madman.

His fumbling, cold fingers yanked the hem of my tight skirt up above my waist. I flinched as his callused fingers dragged along my skin and tugged down my panties.

I heard him spit on his fingers. He knew I wasn't

ready for him. I was never ready anymore. That was how badly I hated him. I kept my legs tight together as he tried to push his fingers between my thighs to lube me with his spit.

"Fucking cunt," he growled. "Piece of trash. You'd still be on the street without me." His thick hand came up on the back of my head, and he shoved me face first toward the desk. I turned to my cheek just in time to avoid breaking my nose.

"Have it your way," he growled. He shoved the spit covered finger into my ass and I squirmed against the hold he had on me. He was damn strong. Even drunk, he was a goddamn beast. It was why everyone was afraid of Ray. I hadn't been afraid. Not until the booze. He couldn't stop the drinking even though it turned him into a raging monster.

My hands slipped forward as he held me against the desk. My fingers grasped for something, anything. My pinky brushed a pen, and I had a brief vision of me stabbing it into Ray's brain. He pushed my feet wide and my arm flung across the blotter. The pen flew off the desk. A smooth marble paperweight rubbed up against my thumb.

Ray stopped. I glanced back hoping he'd somehow decided it wasn't worth the fight. But instead, he had his hand around his cock, desperately milking himself to make himself hard. Tonight the whiskey had been my ally.

While he was staring down at the limp dick in his hand, I grabbed the paperweight. I spun around, and before he had a chance to lift his face, I crowned him on the head. He stumbled back, and his eyes rounded with fury just before they rolled up in his head. He came down like a big tree falling in the forest.

My heart was pounding so hard I was sure it would push open my ribs and hop out of my chest. I didn't stick around to see if he was dead. The paperweight dented the wood floor right next to his head.

I raced to the bedroom and shoved a few things into my backpack. I crept down the hallway and out to the entryway. I kept imagining Ray's thunderous footsteps behind me, but it was my own pulse pounding in my ears. He was out cold. Maybe even dead. I might be spending the rest of my life in jail, but it would be so fucking worth it. Any dank, smelly jail cell would be better than living with Ray.

I opened the front door and ran out into the night. I had nothing and I had nowhere to go, but I couldn't stay one more day.

Creepy swirls of fog curled up around my black boots as I crossed the front lawn. Once I hit the sidewalk, I broke into a run. My hard-soled shoes made the click-clack sound of a flat-footed horse as I ran toward the highway.

Visibility on the road would be minimal, but I was willing to take my chances with oncoming traffic. The heavy mist was a nightly occurrence, a gift from the ocean that coasted in and blanketed the entire area well into the next morning. It brought a bone chill with it that cut right through my thin sweatshirt. I pulled the hood up over my head, covering my nearly white blonde hair with a black sweatshirt and concealing the only thing that might be visible on a night like this.

I looked back once before turning onto the onramp for the two lane highway that would take me the hell out of Wilmington. The turret on Ray's big, gaudy mansion looked like the top of a haunted house beneath the eerie, fog-shrouded glow of the moon. I wouldn't see that house again. I would pull a Cleopatra and stick a poisonous snake down my bra before ever going back there.

A truck's headlights nearly blinded me as the vehicle waddled toward me. With visibility so bad, most cars were moving at a snail's pace. I was glad for that. I pulled the backpack higher on my shoulder and stuck my thumb out hoping the driver had good eyesight and some compassion in his heart.

The truck spit up grit as it pulled off the highway. I raced toward it thinking I could very well have just flagged down a chainsaw murderer like in one of those horror movies. But it didn't even give me pause. It was still better than going back to Ray.

The driver, a middle-aged woman with a curly pile of red hair and a friendly smile, rolled down the window. There were two kids sleeping in the backseat. "Honey, you're practically camouflaged in that black sweatshirt. Where are you heading?"

It wasn't a question I'd prepared for, especially because I had no fucking clue. "I can go as far as you're willing to take me."

She looked at me a second as if she was reconsidering after my shady answer. Then her nice smile popped up. It was a mom smile, the kind some kids, lucky kids, get to see every morning when they head out to the breakfast table. Never got to be one of those lucky kids. "I can get you as far as the marina. But you'll have to ride in back." She motioned to the backseat. "You don't look like a crazy person or murderer, but you understand."

"I'm fine with that. Thanks so much." I ran to the back of the truck, tossed my backpack into the bed and climbed inside. I was free . . . for now.

TWO

COLT

"Sweetheart, if you keep *accidentally* rubbing your hand across my fly, then I'm going to bend you right over this fucking table and take you right in front of all the other bar patrons." Hunter sat back against the vinyl seat, but his threat only worked to make the brunette tease him more. She pressed her tits against his arm and grinned wickedly as her hand disappeared beneath the table.

Hunter growled. "That's it. We're going back to the boat for a few minutes." He gave the brunette a nudge, and she hopped out of the booth. My brother hadn't even bothered to ask her name. He stood up, towering over the petite girl now, and her brown eyes rounded with fear which was quickly replaced by excitement when it seemed to occur to her that a man Hunter's size was going to be equipped with an equally giant dick.

"Thought you were going to bend me over the table," the brunette said coyly, adding a little lip bite for extra effect.

Hunter reached down and shook the table enough to clink the beer glasses together and send beer sloshing over the side of the pitcher.

I steadied the pitcher. "Hey, watch what the fuck you're doing. That's good beer."

Hunter took hold of the girl's hand. "We'll go to the boat. At least when we rock it, the beer won't spill." He led her out of the bar.

Some of the local men, who had been sneering at us from the first second we'd walked in, watched with fury as Hunter led the girl out. But no one would stop him. No one stopped my brother, Hunter, from doing anything he wanted to do. No one stopped any of us Stone brothers. But, there were times when I wished that someone would try.

"Told you the rumors were true about this place," Slade chimed in. "Heard it all over Facebook. Head to Bootlegger's if you want to be surrounded by willing pussy." The jukebox switched over to a Rolling Stone's tune, and it thrummed through the place drowning out the clamor of voices.

"Facebook? What the fuck are you doing on there?"

Slade picked up his beer and took a loud swig before wiping his mouth with the back of his hand. "People post some highly informative things on there."

"Since when are you interested in *informative*?"

"Whenever the bits of information come between nice pictures of tits."

I nodded. "That's more like it."

"Hey, but I didn't tell you," he said. He drank more beer and filtered the liquid through his teeth as if he was tasting fine wine instead of cheap beer. "Parker started a Facebook group page for our 'sticky fingers' contest." He lifted his hand and waved his own fingers in case I wasn't grasping his meaning. Slade could be such a stupid ass sometimes. "You're still at the top with fifty-two. That asshole, Feeney, claims to be only one girl away with fifty-one, but I'd bet my left nut he's lying. No way that dickwad has successfully finger fucked fifty-one girls. I'm in third with forty-four, but I'm determined to catch up to you. Can't stand the thought of having my little brother get more pussy than me, even if it's just a good long finger fuck."

"Shit, you've got my name on that page? I didn't sign on for that. Told you I'd participate in your damn contest only because I know I'll win and I want that five hundred dollar pot. But I don't need it advertised all over the fucking place."

"Relax. We've got code names. You're Smith and

Wesson." He smiled proudly, which meant he'd come up with my secret, sticky finger's name. "You know Colt—Smith and Wesson."

"Yeah, got it."

"Oh, and we added a new feature to the contest. If you can record them screaming your name while their pussy is greedily sucking on your fingers, then you get an extra bonus point. But you've got to have it recorded."

"You and Parker have way too much fucking time on your hands."

Slade stared at something over my shoulder. "Speaking of sticky fingers, those two girls at the bar are giving us the come hither look with their tits."

I glanced back toward the bar. As my eyes searched for the come hither tits, they stopped to look at the girl who'd just walked inside. Silky white blonde bangs stuck out from beneath the black hood of her sweatshirt. A long pair of legs, the kind that would look perfect wrapped around me, stretched down from a short, tight skirt and ended in a pair of short black boots. But it wasn't the incredible body and legs that had my attention. It was her face, beautiful, sad and just begging to be treated right. And I knew just how to do that.

"I'm going to wave them over." I heard Slade talk, but I wasn't really listening. I was busy watching as the girl with boots walked across the floor to the bar. She took off her backpack and fished around for some money.

Slade waved over the other two girls, but the new girl had caught his attention too. He leaned his head over the back of the booth to get a better look at her legs. "Holy fucking hell, I just spotted number forty-five."

My fists clenched the second he said it. Had no fucking clue why, but they had.

The girls with the welcoming tits slid into the booth. "Evening ladies," Slade said.

"I'm Gina and this is Shelly," the one with the nearly see through blouse said. Slade didn't introduce us back. We weren't big on formality, and we didn't need people knowing our names. We were just passing through on business, business that wasn't exactly respectable.

"Can either of you ladies tell me the name of the girl at the bar?" Slade asked. "The one with the black boots and the number forty-five tattooed on her ass." Slade winked at me, and I wanted to throw my fist at him. It was rare for me to ever think about hitting my brother, but I wanted to right then.

"No idea, she's not local," Shelly said, looking sufficiently insulted that Slade had asked. "And I don't see any tattoo."

Already bored, I got up to go to the bathroom.

As I stepped back out into the small, dark hallway,

the girl with the boots was backing down the narrow passage. Her attention was riveted on something out in the bar area, and she seemed to be ducking out of sight from whatever it was.

I glanced through to the bar and saw three men who looked as ugly as they looked mean and who seemed to be looking for someone. My money was on the pretty little thing backing down the hallway.

I stood still, and she slammed right into me. She gasped and swung around, wielding her pillowy soft backpack. It struck me on the shoulder.

I peered down at her. Hell, she had a mouth that could make a dead man's cock stand straight up out of the grave. "If you want to use a backpack as a weapon, you need to at least put in a brick or one of those damn textbooks they made us carry around in high school."

She looked back toward the bar area. The three pumped up assholes were walking through the tables checking people out. Hopefully, Slade wouldn't say something insulting to them, but knowing my brother, there was no way he'd keep his mouth shut.

The trio of self-important badasses swept toward the hallway. The girl dropped her backpack, grabbed my arm and pulled me around to hide her from view. She was pressed between me and the wall when their footsteps landed in the hallway. She reached up with her hand and pulled my face down to hers for a kiss. I shielded her more by putting my arms around her small waist and enveloping her completely in my embrace. She was trembling like a kitten stranded out in the snow. The thugs squeezed past to check out the bathrooms. One of them cleverly mumbled that we should 'get a room'.

The kiss continued. It was an act and felt like one at first, her soft lips pressing urgently and nervously against my mouth. But as it continued, she suddenly seemed more pliable in my arms, some of the fear and tension was melting away. My tongue stroked her upper lip in a silent plea to go deeper. Her lips parted. A tiny moan rolled up from her throat as my tongue pushed in between her lips.

She stiffened again as one of the men said, "now that we're in here, I've got to take a piss. Check out front to see if the bitch is hiding in the parking lot."

Two of the men walked back out. The other stayed in the bathroom. Reluctantly, I pulled my mouth from hers, took her hand and picked up her bag. I led her down to the end of the hallway and turned right toward a storage closet. I turned the knob. It was open. We slipped inside.

"You should be safe in here until they leave," I said. She dropped the bag, leaned back against the wall and her long dark lashes fluttered down to shade her pale cheeks. She looked tired and lost.

I walked up to her and rested my hand on the wall next to her head. She opened her lids and peered up at me with round blue eyes. Could easily get fucking lost in those sapphire blue pools.

I pushed her bangs aside to get a better view of her face. "After a kiss like that, I think I deserve an explanation."

THREE
JADE

I stared up at the man I'd used as a human shield. Why the hell did trouble always follow me? And this guy was definitely trouble, and the worst kind of trouble because he was wrapped up in an incredible package of muscles, ink and heartbreak.

"Sorry, that wasn't really a kiss. I was just smashing my face against yours so that those guys couldn't see me. Thanks again for that." I tried to sidle past him. He stuck his leg between my thighs.

I sucked in a wavering breath. He caught my reaction. The truth was, it had started as an all-business kiss, it was the first thing I could think of when I saw Ray's lap dogs coming toward the hallway. I hadn't really noticed that the guy was incredibly beautiful until after I'd spun him toward me and pushed my mouth up to his. He had kissed back in a way that made me instantly melt in his arms. A skilled kisser with a face and body to match, always a lethal combination.

His hand slipped beneath my skirt. I hadn't seen it coming. The guy was bold as hell and with a hard edge that made him just that much more appealing. I stared unflinchingly at him as he rubbed his fingers across the crotch of my panties. A satisfied smile crossed his face as his fingers touched the moisture, the wetness he'd coaxed from me with his damn kiss.

"See, now those wet panties tell me that it was a real kiss and a good one." He leaned closer. He even smelled strong and tough like aftershave that had been made with leather and iron and musk. Whatever the heck it was, it made my head spin.

He glanced toward the door. "I figure we've got a few minutes until those fools give up and leave this place. What could we possibly do to pass the time?" He pulled the crotch of my panties aside. I tried to squirm away from his touch, but he followed, not in a forceful threatening way but in a patient, persistent way.

He kept one hand braced on the wall as he leaned toward me. In a gesture inconsistent with the dangerous, hard man in front of me, he pressed his free hand gently against my face. "You look like you've been through some shit tonight, darlin'." He lowered his mouth to mine and kissed me. His fingers pushed past the crotch of my panties, and his callused thumb ran over my clit.

I gasped against his mouth and wiggled away from his hand again. His fingers followed. "Shh, relax. I'm going to make some of the dark crap go away." His fingers pushed inside of me. I grabbed his shirt for support as my body gave way to the feel of his hand between my legs. My breaths came in short spurts. An hour ago, I was fighting off vile Ray, the man who I'd lived with for the past three years, but here I was, standing in a utility closet with a complete stranger's fingers jammed in my pussy, and I didn't want him to stop. His skill with his mouth and tongue was rivaled by his talented fingers. He knew exactly where to touch and with just the right amount of pressure and attention. His thumb strummed my clit like a fine instrument while his finger fucked me with a perfect, solid rhythm that made my grasp on his shirt tighten.

I rocked my hips to grind harder against his fingers. I was in complete delirium at the notion of this hot guy making me come in the center of a utility closet, and all while Ray's minions were out scouring the parking lot for me.

The man's green eyes faded to chalky gray as his attention to my pussy seemed to be giving him erotic pleasure too. With solid determination, he teased my pussy bringing me closer and closer to climax.

I was just a few strokes away and desperate to finish when the door opened. I should have jolted in alarm or shame but I didn't. I was in a fucking trance. His fingers and the way he stared at me with those pale eyes held me captive.

Another face appeared through the haze. It was a man equally tall and handsome but with darker eyes and lighter hair. His brother, I thought to myself as I continued to move against his hand. The green eyed man's concentration had not been broken either.

"Figures you snagged her before I could even introduce myself," the other man said. "Nice." He stared down at his brother's hand between my legs. "And not a stroke missed, you dawg. Proud to call you my brother. Now finish this because Hunter needs us."

He was having a conversation and his brother was watching and somehow it didn't matter. I was completely determined to finish this or die from disappointment. He was like a fucking pussy wizard. Magical.

"Is Hunter in trouble?" my captor asked, without missing a beat.

"Nope, but the guy he's pounding is."

"I guess that's fifty-fucking-three, you cocksure, sticky fingers pro. You've got this contest in the bag." His footsteps pounded the cement floor and the door shut.

I opened my eyes and gazed at the man. I didn't

even know his name, the beautiful man with the magical fingers. He knew my pussy better than me. My lips parted with an appreciative mewl, and he pressed his mouth against mine. "Come for me, darlin'. I want to watch your incredible face as your pussy clenches around my hand."

The dirty words pushed me right over. My fingers were white as I held tightly to the fabric of his shirt. I cried out as waves of pleasure coursed through my body. Slowly, he pulled his hand from between my legs. I collapsed against his chest and he held me. For a brief second, I felt safe, as if everything in my world wasn't completely fucked.

I was finally steady enough on my feet to stand straight on my own. "So, I was part of a contest?" I asked. "Number fifty-fucking-three? Does it always have to be in a utility closet or are there other exotic locations on the list?"

He smiled. "Closet is optional. There's a five hundred dollar pot, but—" He leaned closer and kissed me. "Contest or not, I would have done that. You looked like you needed it."

I reached up and pushed his long, black hair behind his ear. He had a sliver plug in each lobe. That, coupled with his size, mass of tattoos and black hair, definitely made him look like someone you would run from in a dark alley. Only I hadn't run. I'd spread my legs for him with hardly a second thought. I hadn't even minded when his brother watched. Had I been living such a dissolute life as Ray's plaything that my modesty had been shaken completely away? Or was this man just that good? I held on to the hope that it was the latter.

As I reached back to pull up my hood, my sleeve dropped down. My utility closet fantasy man took hold of my wrist and turned it to get a better look at the bruises Ray had left on my forearm. His face turned grim. As menacing as he'd looked before with his massive shoulder span, dark hair and silver-green eyes, now he looked positively lethal.

"Which one of those guys did this to you?" The question slid from between a tight jaw.

I shook my head. "No, it wasn't them." I pulled my arm away and pushed the sleeve down. I'd just let him bring me to orgasm, and I didn't even know his name. I didn't feel the need to expose myself any more to the man. He was just one stranger in what I figured would be a long line of them on my way to finding a safe place for myself. Although, I doubted that I would cross paths with many who looked like the stranger in front of me.

He walked to the door. I could have asked his name, but it would be easier to forget him if I didn't know it. He opened the door and peered out. The music had stopped, and only a few sounds rumbled up the hallway. They sounded like grunts of pain.

He glanced back. His eyes were now pale gray beneath the yellowish light bulb hanging over the doorway. "I think if you keep up your hood and make a wide berth around the action in the center of the bar, you can slip right past the three goons. One is already face down on the ground, and my brothers are taking care of the others."

He flashed me a smile and walked out into the hallway. I yanked on my backpack, pulled the hood low over my head and ducked my face down. We stepped into the barroom just as Grady, one of Ray's most loyal guards, pulled a shiny blade from under his coat. In one fluid movement, the handsome stranger grabbed Grady's wrist and wrenched his arm painfully behind him. The knife fell to the floor along with Grady. The brother who had come into the closet was standing with his foot on Belkin's head, another one of Ray's watch dogs. He was reading text messages, looking bored, as another man, who was also startlingly handsome and even bigger than my closet lover, pounded a pig faced guy named Tuttle into ground beef.

The other patrons stood at the far end of the bar watching in awe as the three brothers destroyed Ray's men. I slipped out the door and looked around. I needed to make a quick decision, so I could get out of sight.

I headed toward the docks thinking I could hide out on a boat for the night. I could be up at the crack of dawn, before anyone came down to the marina. My feet sounded incredibly loud on the salt and wind weathered planks of the dock. I was halfway when I realized that there were other footsteps pounding the dock behind me. I twisted around and stumbled back.

All I saw was the ugly lump on Ray's head as he lunged at me and grabbed hold of my throat. The only thing he needed to look more rabid was foam frothing from his mouth. I was a dead woman. I couldn't breathe. Panic set in as his fingers squeezed my neck, blocking my air passage. I backed up and he followed. Tears burned my eyes. I clawed at his arm, leaving long thin trails of blood as my fingernails took skin.

"I was good to you, and this is how you repay me?" he sneered.

The dark fog in my head was much blacker than the surrounding air. I was losing consciousness. My eyes darted toward the bar hoping to see someone come out. But the lights on the marina were shrouded by fog. It would have been hard to see two figures struggling on the pier.

I had never been afraid of dying, but having Ray take pleasure in it was too much. I didn't want to die by his hand. With my last bit of strength and clarity, I swung my leg up. It landed between Ray's legs, and my knee slammed his balls. Before doubling over in agony, he shoved me hard.

I coughed and gasped for air as I fell back. My head smacked the edge of the dock as I rolled into the water. Icy saltwater made me suck in a sharp breath again. My air passages were swollen. I desperately sucked in the cold night air, all the while trying to stay above the surface. The water swirled black and frigid around me. Somewhere in the fall, I'd lost my backpack. I heard Ray cussing from above. I ducked under the water and swam around the boats. The ocean was scary enough in broad daylight, but in the shroud of a foggy night, it was terrifying. I had to push away the idea that sea creatures with jagged teeth and long stingers were watching me from the shadowy depths.

The lack of oxygen and the icy water slowed my arms and legs down as if I was moving through tar. Ray was stomping along the pier. I could hear him, but I couldn't see him. I was sure the boats and fog were hiding me too. Gritty salt water smacked me in the face. I sucked some in and started coughing again. I covered my mouth to stifle the sound, but treading water with one numb arm wasn't easy. I grabbed onto a rope ladder that was hanging off the back of a weathered looking trawler. My fingers were so numb, I could barely feel the rough rope beneath them.

I was shivering so hard my teeth clacked together and my entire body shook. My neck ached as if it had been wrung out like a wet towel. If I hadn't kicked the bastard in the balls, I would be dead, floating in the water, waiting to become fish food.

Ray had been a handsome, charismatic twenty-four-year-old when he'd pulled me from the streets. I was a teenage runaway with no home, no money and no hopes of ever seeing my adult years. He was making good money at what I later found out was an illegal book-making business. But even when I discovered his secret, it hadn't bothered me. People weren't being hurt or killed by his business. The only crime was people losing their money on crappy bets. I figured I was no one to judge. I'd had to do a lot of shitty things myself to stay alive. But it wasn't long before I discovered the sinister side of Ray's business, the ugly consequences when someone didn't pay up. And as Ray's business grew, his temper and propensity for violence grew with it. When the drinking grew out of control, I knew it was time for me to get away from him for good.

I clung to the rope ladder, hiding myself beneath the shadow of the fishing boat. The choppy current smacked me up against the hull more than once, but I was almost too numb to feel it. A weird, sleepy feeling pushed down on my skull as if it was a heavy hand trying to shove me beneath the water. For a second, my eyes drifted shut. They felt too heavy to open.

A splash of seawater in my face shocked me awake again. My body temperature was dropping. I knew if a stayed in the water, I would eventually lose consciousness.

I'd lost track of Ray's footsteps. The ladder hung off the side near the stern. I hoped the fog would cloak me enough. The thin cotton sweatshirt was amazingly heavy when it was soaked with water. My feet, still tucked in the boots and sloshing in their own pools of water, managed to find the bottom rung. With all my strength, I hoisted myself out of the water.

I glanced around. A quiet boat marina was an eerie sight on a foggy night. The coast line was completely obliterated by the silvery haze. It felt like I was on a strange planet all by myself. Since they'd all gone to sleep for the night, even the usual clatter of seabirds was missing. I couldn't hear any music or voices coming from Bootlegger's.

In my exhausted state of agony, my mind floated back to him, the man who'd dragged me into the utility closet. He and his brothers were pounding Ray's men, men who were known for being ruthless and brutal. But they sure couldn't stand up to the three brothers.

I pulled myself onto the deck. The trembling was almost uncontrollable now. I stumbled around looking for something to protect myself with in case Ray spotted me. It was obvious he wasn't going to be satisfied until he killed me. There was a metal tool box bolted to the wall below the pilot house. I opened it and reached in for the first thing I saw, a deadly sharp fillet knife.

I walked around behind the pilot house, back to where the nets were piled. They looked surprisingly neat and new compared to the rest of the boat, as if they'd hardly ever been used.

I scrunched down into a ball, shielded by the wall behind me and the pile of nets in front of me. Soaked through to the bone, I doubted I would be able to stop the shivering, but at least I was out of the water. I gripped the knife in my numb fingers and hugged myself tightly. The heavy, unnatural groggy feeling overtook me again. I couldn't keep my eyes open any longer.

FOUR
COLT

The rest of the bar patrons had stood by without interfering as we smeared the place with the three assholes. After one had said something harsh to the girls sitting with Slade, my mouthy brother had told them to go home and blow each other. That was all it took.

Hunter had walked in just as Slade was being dragged out of the booth by all three of them. That was the beginning of a really bad night for those three. The other people in the bar seemed to know the guys, and no one felt the urge to help them. It would have been the same for Hunter, Slade and me if we'd been at our local bar and someone had come in and beat the shit out of us. Of course, I didn't see that happening anytime soon.

The three men were about as wrecked as they could

be, so we left the bar, figuring it was time to get back to the boat and back home. As we walked out of the bar, a man who looked vaguely familiar and who was holding his crotch and cussing as if someone had just kicked him in the balls, staggered past us. He seemed to be looking for someone.

"If you're looking for three pussies who think they know how to fight, head inside." Hunter pointed back with his thumb.

The man stopped to stare at us for a second and then hobbled inside with his sore nuts.

"I know that guy," Slade said.

"He's a bookie. I've used him for laying down bets on fights and football games. Haven't used him for awhile. He's a real suave piece of shit." Hunter pulled out a cigarette. "Shit, my knuckles hurt. Is there still some ice in the chest?"

"Probably. Speaking of ice, it's cold as hell out here." I looked around wondering where the girl had gone. It wasn't a great night to be out. That's when it occurred to me, the bookie must have been looking for the girl. He might even have been the one to leave the bruises on her arm. He was lucky he was already out of my reach as I put those little puzzle pieces together. I would have loved to have left his face print on the bar counter.

"Visibility is pretty bad out there," Slade said. "You think the light is going to be enough in this pea soup?"

I jumped onto deck first. "Should be fine because we'll be the only people stupid enough to be out in pea soup."

Hunter hopped onboard and went toward the pilot house for ice. He stopped at the tool box. "Who left the tool box open?"

"Wasn't me," Slade said as he untied the line from the cleat.

"Don't look at me," I said.

"Shit, my fillet knife is missing." Hunter leaned down and fished through the box. He straightened and looked around. "Someone must have climbed onboard and robbed us. Good thing we got rid of our cargo before we stopped for drinks."

"We might be stupid enough to take the boat out with zero visibility, but if we're ever stupid enough to leave twenty thousand dollars of cocaine on our boat while we slip into a bar for beer—" Slade started, but Hunter held up his hand to silence him.

My gaze followed Hunter's. A line of wet puddles led from the stern and disappeared behind the pilot house. I looked at him and he nodded. Slade climbed onboard. The three of us rounded the pilot house ready to take on our stowaway.

A small figure was huddled down in the shadowy pile of nets. The person didn't move or flinch, even with our heavy footsteps making the deck creak. I walked over and kicked the bottom of the person's shoe.

Our stowaway jumped up with a gasp of terror. The sharp, gleaming blade of the fillet knife arced around as she swung her arm wildly at me.

I leaned back away from the tip of the blade and then snatched the girl's wrist. "You're going to hurt someone with that thing, darlin'."

She kicked toward my knee but missed. The sudden movement had pushed the hood from her sweatshirt off her head. Her light blonde hair nearly glowed white in the weak moonlight.

"Hey, it's number fifty-three," Slade said from behind me.

The girl's blue eyes darted back and forth as if she had no idea where she was. She held the knife firmly in front of her, but it was obvious she hardly had the strength to stand, let alone stab someone.

I stepped closer. She backed up. "Hey, it's all right. We're not going to hurt you."

She seemed to recognize my voice. "It's you," she said in a weak, sad whisper. A violent tremble started in her hands, and she dropped the knife. She swayed on her feet, and her long lashes fluttered down. Her knees gave out. I lunged forward and caught her.

"Do you know her?" Hunter asked.

"This is the girl those assholes were looking for." I

lifted her into my arms. "Need to get her up to the pilot house and under a blanket. Her skin feels like ice." I glanced back at Slade. "Are we about ready to shove off?"

"Yep."

"Good, let's get out of here before they come looking for her."

I carried our beautiful and very cold stowaway up to the pilot house. Hunter followed. The girl was shaking hard as I pressed her against me, hoping my body heat would help.

Hunter pulled out the emergency kit. "I think we've got one of those weird foil blankets in here. Supposed to be good for keeping people warm. Or at least that's what I've seen in movies." He pulled out a cellophane package and ripped it open.

"I've got to get her out of these wet clothes." I lowered her onto the bench running along the back wall of the pilot house. Her heavy lids opened, and she stared at me. With the exception of her pink cheeks, her skin was much paler than it had been when I'd had her warm and in my arms back in the bar.

I crouched down in front of her. "What's your name, darlin'?"

She blinked slowly as if she was trying to figure out the answer to my question. The hypothermia had really worked a number on her. "Jade," she said. It seemed to take all her energy.

"Jade? Pretty name. I've got to take your wet clothes off, Jade, so we can wrap you in our special foil wrapper." I unlaced her boots and slid them off her feet.

She stared down at my hand as I unzipped her sweatshirt. "How did you find me?" she asked.

"I didn't. You found me." I slipped the sweatshirt off her shoulders. Hunter started the engine. The dim bulbs of the pilot house flickered overhead but didn't give much light. Still, it would have been impossible not to notice the red lines on her neck.

She winced as I reached up and touched her neck. "That bookie, the one who sent the thugs to find you, did he do this?"

Her throat moved with a swallow, and her eyes shut with the pain. She didn't answer me, and it wasn't my business. Of course, that didn't mean that I wouldn't fucking kill the guy the next time we crossed paths.

I reached for the t-shirt she was wearing. She pulled back from my touch. "I don't want to be fifty-four too. Please. I just don't want to feel anything for the rest of the night." Tears pooled in her eyes.

I stroked her cheek. "I need to get you warm. That's all. I promise." She lifted her arms as if there were heavy weights hanging from the ends of them. I pulled her shirt off but left the lacy pink bra. "Let's shimmy this skirt off of you. Panties can stay." I unbuttoned her skirt. She leaned against me for support as I slid off the wet fabric.

Hunter helped me wrap her in the foil blanket. A faint smile crossed her face as she watched us. "I feel like a roast going into an oven." She looked at me. "An oven, damn, that sounds so darn good right now. I'd just slather myself in butter and crawl inside."

I touched her bottom lip. "At least your teeth aren't chattering anymore."

Slade came up to the pilot house and grinned as he held up a bottle of whiskey. "Nothing like a swig of liquid fire to heat up the blood."

He unscrewed the top and held it out. Jade lifted her arm out of the blanket and took hold of it. Her face scrunched up as she drank the whiskey.

"I don't know if I've ever seen someone look so damn cute drinking whiskey," Slade said.

She pressed her hand against her mouth and concentrated on swallowing. Then she took a deep breath. "That's really awful." She leaned back in her foil wrap. "But thank you. I feel better already."

She held up the bottle, but Slade put out his palm. "Keep it. You might need more."

The engine rumbled and the boat vibrated as we got to open water. I glanced through the windows. Chalky gray fog clouded the view. The light on the bow looked like a ball of fire in the thick, cold mist.

Jade took another few drinks of whiskey and handed me the bottle. I took a few swallows and put it down on the ground. The thin foil crinkled around our saltwater drenched stowaway. Even cold, shivering and miserable she was incredible.

She scooted closer to me. "I don't want to sound greedy, seeing as how you guys shared your giant burrito wrapper with me and everything, but can I have some more of your body heat?"

"I think I've got some to spare."

She crawled onto my lap and pressed her face against my chest. It made my throat tighten as if someone had clamped fingers around it. I couldn't remember the last time something had produced a lump in my throat. Emotion, feelings and, hell, even love had been turned off in all of us Stone brothers long ago. You couldn't grow up with our father and have emotions. There was just way too much pain. We stopped feeling and life got easier. But holding this girl, a girl who seemed to have a pretty fucked up life too, made my throat ache. I tightened my arms around her.

She clamped the silver blanket shut with her hand and adjusted her bottom in my lap. "So, what was she like?"

I looked down at her. "What was who like?"

"Lucky number one." She yawned, closed her eyes and rested her head against me. Instinctively, my arms tightened their hold, and all I could think was that I wanted to protect her. "Fifty-three sucks. I want to be lucky number one." Her body stopped trembling. She relaxed in my arms and fell fast asleep.

FIVE

JADE

The evening had been a blur, the nightmarish events swirled in with a green eyed stranger who was anything but a nightmare. The same man was stretched out next to me under the blanket. The drop in body temperature and shots of whiskey had knocked me nearly senseless. I'd slept soundly in his arms as the fishing trawler crept back to their hometown marina. I vaguely remembered lifting my head to look around, only to be met with the same thick fog we'd traveled through. But the town smelled different. It smelled lighter, less oppressive, but I was sure that was only because I was now a good distance away from Ray.

I stared over at the man. I still hadn't even learned his name. He had a beautiful profile to go with the rest of his beautiful self. The night before, he had carried me all the way from the marina to their truck as if I weighed nothing more than the crinkly silver blanket I was wrapped in. After I'd nearly frozen to death in the ocean, his body heat had felt like the greatest, most luxurious blanket, and I couldn't bear to part with it. I'd clung to him like a barnacle on a ship hull. And after he lowered me onto his bed, in the shadows of his room, I watched him strip down to his boxer briefs. Heat had swirled through my body then too, but a different kind of heat, like the kind that had washed over me in the utility closet when he'd boldly pressed his hand between my legs. His finely chiseled arms, shoulders and stomach had become part of my dreams. I had been weak and out of it, but he hadn't tried anything. Instead, he'd stretched out under the cover and wrapped me in that same delicious body heat, making me feel as if I'd never be cold again.

Daylight was pouring in through the tattered curtains covering his window. It was a sparsely furnished room, with a single, equally tattered dresser. There was a chair that looked as if it had seen better days sitting in front of a desk that had a laptop and nothing more. Dirty clothes and socks on the floor made me pretty confident that he didn't have a woman living with him. But I was sure plenty of them had passed through his bedroom door. Possibly even fifty-two.

The bed creaked as he turned, and his big arm came

down across me. His eyes popped open as if he'd suddenly remembered I was there. His eye color changed according to the light shining on them. This morning they were more green than gray, and they were spectacular.

"Hey, it's my saltwater soaked angel. How are you feeling?"

"Better. Thanks to your body heat."

"Happy to share." He grew quiet. We both did. A warm tension filled the small space between us. Beneath the covers he reached across and trailed his callused fingers along my side. My breath was immediately ragged as I thought about the night before when, in the middle of my stressful evening, he'd so deftly made me come. And in a utility closet, no less. Now those magical hands and fingers were under the covers with me, and we were dressed only in our underwear. There was no way to tell myself anything different. I wanted him to touch me again.

He must have sensed it. He watched my face over the pillow, either for my reaction or a sign that I wanted him to stop, as his fingers slid my bra strap off my shoulder. He pulled it down to expose my breast. Then his gaze dropped from my face to my chest.

"Hmm, had a feeling they'd be as hot as the rest of you." He teased my nipple between his thumb and forefinger, and I drew in a stuttering breath. All I could think about was the way those fingers had strummed my pussy so perfectly; I could think of nothing else but reaching climax. Even when his brother had walked in on us, my mind had been too set on finishing to care.

He leaned over and pressed his mouth against my nipple, still teasing it but now using his teeth and tongue. From the way my body reacted, it was obvious that his magic skills went way beyond his hands. I reached up and tangled my fingers in his long black hair and held his face closer to me.

Heat swirled through me, and my pussy pulsed with moisture. The entire thing was surreal. I was no longer in Ray's control. I knew I wasn't free of him, but for the moment, I was away from him. And now I was in a strange room, in a strange town, and I was readily submitting to a guy whose name I didn't even know. That thought suddenly struck me as funny. I laughed.

He pulled my nipple between his lips before releasing it. He looked up at me. "Have to say, I don't usually get that reaction when I have a nipple between my teeth."

"It's just— I don't even know your name. It seemed kind of comical. Or maybe it was just a nervous laugh."

"I'm Colton but people call me Colt." He reached up to shake hands.

I put my hand in his. "Nice to meet you. I'm Jade."

He gripped my hand and pulled me against his hard

body. "Very fucking nice to meet you, Jade." He leaned his mouth toward mine.

The bedroom door burst open, and a girl with short copper hair and a pretty face, who looked as if she'd lived a hard life and weathered it all with confidence, strolled in. She had a tiny gold hoop in her nose and a tattoo of a dragonfly on her neck. I pulled away from Colt's arms.

Colt rolled onto his back and covered his eyes with his forearm. "Fuck, Street, why the hell are you in here?"

She winked at me as she crawled on top of him straddling his hips with long, suntanned thighs. Her midriff top barely covered the bottom of her bra. "Come on, Colt, you always love to see my bright smiling face in the morning."

He lowered his arm. "No, I fucking don't. Especially this morning."

His words didn't make her leave or even take pause for a second. "Hunter said you had a new friend who might need some clothes to wear." She reached over and held out her hand. "I'm Amy, by the way. Not Street." She smacked Colt's chest, and he flinched. "They've called me Street Corner Girl since I was twelve. I used to sell lemonade on the street corner to try and earn a little cash. And when nobody bought lemonade, I started selling kisses. Earned enough for a bicycle. But the Stone brothers have never let me forget it. Even though they were my best customers."

I pulled my arm from the covers. "I'm Jade."

Amy's brow creased. She wriggled her ass on top of Colt. She reached between her legs and rubbed her palm over the blanket. "Oh wow, Colt, you should do something about ole Mr. Woody here."

"Yeah, that's what I was working on before you burst in here with your annoying sing-song voice."

Amy was bold and funny and I already liked her. She reached down and grabbed the blanket. Before I could protest, she yanked it back and surveyed my body. "Yep, looks like we wear the same size."

"Yep, you're fucking identical," Colt said. "Only she has tits in a place where you just have two dots like someone drew them in with a pencil."

"Someone is extra mean and grumpy this morning." Amy released the cover, and I pulled it back over me.

"I wonder why. Now get out," Colt said.

"Yes, sir." Amy looked at me. "I stuck your boots out in the sun to dry. Those are cool. I've always wanted a pair like that."

"Thanks, that was really nice of you. They're my favorite."

Amy climbed off and sifted through some of the dirty clothes on the floor. She pressed one t-shirt to her face, breathed in and scrunched up her face in disgust. She tossed it at Colt. "Shit, you need to burn that one."

"Street, I swear to god I'm going to—"

She totally ignored him and picked up another shirt. She pressed it to her face. "It'll have to do." She tossed it to me. "Put this on. You look hungry."

"I could eat," I said.

"Good, I brought some muffins. Do you like blueberry muffins? These guys don't. They don't like anything that isn't covered in bacon grease and hot sauce."

"I like muffins." I sat up to pull on the shirt.

Colt propped himself up on his elbows and glared at Amy. "I need to put a fucking lock on that door."

I pulled on the t-shirt.

"Looks good," Amy said. "Let's go."

Colt looked up at me. I shrugged and kissed his forehead. "Thanks again for the body heat."

"Fucking great." He collapsed back.

I followed Amy out to the kitchen. The kitchen was smaller than Ray's walk-in closet. Of course a primping rooster like Ray had an unusually big collection of clothes. He'd had an extra large closet built to accommodate his fashion obsession. That was something that had always made me cringe— his time in front of the mirror. Once I'd told him he was like a thirteen-year-old girl with the way he was always standing in front of the mirror. He'd backhanded me before I had a chance to move out of his reach. My lips swelled up, and I'd never teased him again. But inside my head, I was always having a good laugh.

Four mismatched chairs, one with a leg that was duct taped in several places, sat around a plastic table, the kind you'd find out on a patio instead of inside a kitchen. Dishes were piled high, and rather than wash them, someone had bought an extra large package of paper plates. There was a white bakery bag in the center of the table and a Styrofoam cup with steaming coffee.

"Pull up a chair, but avoid that one." She pointed to the one with tape. "Do you want some coffee?"

"That'd be great."

"Don't be shy. Grab a muffin. You'll find in this house, if you don't get grabby with the food, you'll end up with crumbs." She turned to the sink and rinsed a cup out. She sat down across from me and poured half the coffee into the cup.

"Do you live here?" I asked.

"Me? God no. Not that my place is any better. I'm the neighbor. I live with my mom. She's loco, but she stays out of my way, and I make sure she doesn't do anything nutty like stick her head in the oven." She propped one foot on the chair and picked at the muffin she'd pulled from the bag. She was bone thin and there were circles under her light brown eyes, but even then, she was extremely pretty.

She reached up to her neck and swiped her fingers across it to remind me of the marks left behind by Ray's hands. "Are you on the run from an abusive man?"

I nodded and took a bite of muffin.

"Looks like a good decision. Nothing worse than living with a sonavabitch. My mom and I did for ten years and then my dad fell off his fishing boat. I tried not to smile when they came to the door to tell us. But, it was better, you know? These guys had the same problem. We all grew up together figuring out ways to dodge our old men." She lowered her voice. "They had it a lot worse. Did you see Colt's back?"

I was confused. "No, why?"

"You'll know when you see it. They've all got the same scars. I still remember them showing up to school on an icy winter day without coats and socks. I at least had a coat. I was living like royalty compared to the Stone brothers."

"Hey, Street—" I could already recognize Colt's deep, smooth voice, and I realized it fit him perfectly.

"Yeah, what?" she called back as she took a joint from her pocket.

"Shut up, I'm trying to sleep," Colt replied.

"Yeah, all right." She leaned forward. "Colt doesn't like it when I talk about stuff like that. They're all assholes, and they hop from girl to girl, but none of them would lift a hand to one. Even with their shitty childhood, and with the shady crap they're into, they wouldn't hurt a woman. I love that about them. The rest of the town is scared of them, but I think they also kind of admire them, you know? It's a small town and a lot of people have lived here forever. They know how it was for them." She lit the joint and squinted at me through the smoke before offering me some. I shook my head.

She held the smoke in while she talked through her teeth. "What are you going to do now?" She released the breath, and the strong sage-like aroma of weed filled the kitchen.

I broke off a chunk of muffin. "Not too sure. I left with just a backpack, and I even lost that."

"That's right. I was going to get you some clothes. Yours are still on the porch with your boots, but you're going to need something to wear. I'll go home and grab a few things."

"That's really cool of you, Amy. I'll get them back to you just as soon as I can."

"Street—" this was a different deep voice. "I've got a problem."

"We all know that, Hunter." She rolled her eyes, but I could tell her expression had changed with the sound of Hunter's deep voice.

"Street Corner, don't toy with me. You know the problem I'm talking about."

"You've got two hands, don't ya? And you only need one cause it's not big enough for two." She pushed another piece of muffin through her lips.

I smiled. "Are you Hunter's girlfriend?"

She laughed, but there was a sadness behind it. "Hell no, the last thing I need is a headache like Hunter Stone." She said it with confidence, but it was obvious there was more to it. "Nope, these boys are nothing but trouble when it comes to your heart." She pointed at me with the joint between her fingers and inclined her head toward the hallway. "Especially pretty boy in there. Remember that, in case you're thinking about getting yourself wrapped up with him."

This time it was my sad laugh that rolled across the wobbly plastic table. "Don't worry. Like you said— the last thing I need at the moment." I leaned back. "What I need is a job. You wouldn't happen to know of something?"

She sat forward and smacked her hand on the table. "Do I ever? I work at Lazy Daze Bar, and the other girl who I worked with got married and left. The owner's a cranky old man, but he'll hire you if you're interested. The pay sucks and you have to work until two in the morning, but the tips make up for it. What do you think?"

"Great. I'm just not sure where to stay. Is there a park or something nearby?" My life on the streets was going to come in handy now.

"You can't stay in the park. The local police will run you out of there. I know from experience. My mom's too crazy, otherwise I'd take you in. But these guys will let you stay, I'm sure of it. It's a mess and they're all pigs, but it's a roof."

"Who are you calling pigs?" Loud footsteps pounded the hallway floor. I looked back. It was Hunter. He was even bigger than Colt. He was wearing only boxer briefs, and an extremely anxious looking erection.

"I'm calling you boys, pigs." She laughed as he stepped into view. "Holy crap, maybe you do need two hands this morning."

"Nope, I just need my Street Corner girl. Now hop on." He turned his back to her, but not before I glimpsed the scars on his skin. Amy held onto the lit joint as she climbed up onto his back. She stuck the joint in between his lips, and he took a hit.

Amy looked tiny on his back. She rested her chin on his shoulder. I could see it right then as she held onto him that she had a big thing for him. "Hey, Jade is going to stay with you guys for awhile. Just until she earns some money. Then we're going to get an apartment together." She winked at me.

"Who's Jade?" Hunter asked. He had the same jet black hair as Colt but his eyes were dark brown.

Amy rolled her eyes. "The girl sitting at your elegant kitchen table."

"Oh yeah. That's fine." He headed out of the kitchen with Amy clinging to his back.

"I'll bring you some clothes. We can go over to the bar later to meet the owner," Amy said as she passed by.

"Sounds great." I looked around at the messy little kitchen. I was safe for now, but I couldn't leech off these guys for long. Somehow, I was going to have to figure out how to survive without ending up back on the streets.

SIX
COLT

I pulled on some shorts and walked out to the empty kitchen. Slade had gone out fishing for the day. He was the only brother who liked to fish and he hired himself out to the other fishing boats when our business was slow. Hunter had shit to do on his motorcycle.

After Amy had come in and lured Jade from my bed with a blueberry muffin, I'd gone back to sleep, thoroughly disappointed and a little lonely. Something about having her in my bed all night, even if nothing more happened than me sharing my body heat with her, felt right. I'd missed her almost as soon as she left, a completely foreign feeling for me.

The kitchen sparkled. The dishes had been washed, dried and put away. The dish washing culprit had even taken the time to find a few straggly flowers from somewhere in our barren front yard. They sat in a glass of water looking slightly wilted and completely out of place in our kitchen. At some point during my late morning doze, Hunter had stuck his head in my bedroom door to let me know our stowaway was staying with us for awhile. Not sure why he had to let me know. I would have asked her to stay anyhow. It was obvious she had no place to go and no money to help her out. Since I'd never seen either of my brothers clean the kitchen, I was pretty sure our new housemate had cleaned up.

I heard the bathroom sink running. The door was ajar, and as I knocked, the door pushed open. Jade was still wearing my t-shirt as she leaned over the sink washing out her lacy pink bra and panties. She had her wet hair in one long braid down the center of her back. Something told me that she'd spent more than one day cleaning her clothes in a gas station bathroom.

She looked back at me and smiled.

"You look a lot better than last night," I said. "Guess you're feeling better."

"I am, thanks to you guys." She turned off the sink and faced me. "I hope you don't mind. These are all I've got. Amy was going to bring me some shorts and a shirt, but I think asking her to share her underwear might be asking too much."

"She'd do it if you asked. That's just the way Street

is. She doesn't have much herself, but she's always ready to help everyone."

"I only just met her, and I already think she's awesome."

"Yeah, I liked her a little more before this morning. But she's like a sister."

"Really? Your brother wasn't treating her like a sister this morning."

"Hunter? Yeah, that's a whole complicated thing. Not really sure what's going on there. I know Street likes him and I'm pretty sure if my brother ever really thought about it, he'd discover that he likes her too. But for now, she's just Street. Any of us would risk our lives for her, and there aren't many people I can say that about."

"She's lucky to have you guys. And I am too. I promise I won't be a burden for long." She hung her bra up over the shower. I was still recuperating from the disappointing morning. I was getting hard just watching her hang her underwear up to dry. Didn't help that the bottom of her perfect ass poked out from beneath my shirt as she lifted her arms to reach up to the shower curtain bar.

"You're no burden. I'll bet you're not half as expensive to feed as Slade. And it's kind of nice seeing a lacy bra hanging over the shower rod." I stepped up behind her and brushed my fingers over the naked skin on her ass.

Her soft gasp bounced off the shower tile. She turned and my arms went around her, but I could tell there was some resistance, as if her body was saying yes and her head was saying no.

I lowered my arms.

She peered up at me with those blue eyes that I already couldn't stop thinking about. "I'm sorry, Colt, it's just that—" She looked down at the bruises on her arm.

I pushed up her chin with my fingers. "No apologies. You've gone through some shit, and now's not the time. Not going to lie, I'm disappointed, but I get it. How about I run you to the store and you can pick up some things? It's going to get old walking around in wet panties all the time." I stopped and shook my head. "Wow, that didn't sound right coming out of my mouth at all."

She laughed and picked up my hand. My knuckles were still swollen from the fight at Bootlegger's. "I really can't thank you enough for letting me stay here." Her voice wavered.

I reached up to her face just as the bathroom door popped open and smacked me on the shoulder.

Amy was standing in the hallway with a giant smile and some clothes.

"Fucking hell, Street, did you wake up this morning and immediately plan out how to annoy the shit out of me today?"

She pushed past me. "Yeah, that' right, you egotistical butt face, I wake up every morning with your name on my lips." She made a dramatic show of stretching and yawning. "Oh yay, it's a new day. I wonder what that dream boat Colt is up to. He's the center of the fucking universe, after all." She turned to Jade. "Here, I think these will work for now." Amy turned around and shooed me out.

SEVEN
JADE

Amy's shirt was exceptionally small across the chest and, without a bra, I ended up walking through the entire store with my arms crossed over my breasts. And without any underwear, her shorts were riding up uncomfortably too. Occasionally, I withdrew one hand from my boobs to pull at the hem of the shorts and wrench them from my crotch. Colt was entertained.

"I'm glad you find this amusing," I said. "Thank goodness someone was smart enough to invent underwear."

"Really? I say fuck 'em. Just one more obstacle, as far as I'm concerned."

Colt looked completely out of place in the small store, and it seemed not many people were used to seeing him in there. His black t-shirt made his tattoos look particularly menacing as they trailed out along his arms. The overhead lights flickered reflections off his pale eyes and the silver plugs. One particularly frightened woman grabbed her little girl's hand and pulled her out of the shoe aisle when she saw us come around the corner. Colt didn't seem to notice or care.

He looked down at my feet. I'd pulled on the boots even though they were still moist. "What size are you?"

"You don't have to buy me shoes too. The underwear, shorts and shirts are enough."

"You can't walk around in those boots all the time. Although, I did have this really great dream last night, and those black boots were an important character."

I blushed. "Holy shit, if you could earn money flirting you'd be a rich man."

"See, and I consider myself a rich man just because I'm damn good at flirting. Among other things."

"I'm not going to argue there." I hid another blush, while also still trying to hide my very exposed breasts.

"Anything else?"

"I hate to ask for anything more . . . but a toothbrush and a few bathroom essentials?"

"That makes sense. You'll have to excuse me, I've never brought home a stray girl before."

I took hold of his arm. He stared down at my fingers

on his arm and then gazed up at me with a look that made me wonder why the hell I'd turned him down earlier. He was something else.

"I'll pay you back for all this just as soon as I can. Amy is going to introduce me to her boss later this afternoon."

"She's trying to get you a gig at Lazy Daze? That place is a hell hole. Of course, we spend a lot of time there, but we sort of fit well in a hell hole. You don't."

"Trust me, I just left hell behind. Every place else is going to feel like heaven."

He gazed down at me long enough to send my heart a few good paces ahead. He stirred every inch of me. "Glad you got free of him."

"Yeah, me too." I knew I wasn't completely free of Ray, but for now, the feeling of relief at not having to see him or talk to him or have him touch me was nearly overwhelming. I hadn't realized just how badly I needed to leave him until now. It was as if I could finally release the breath I'd been holding for the last year.

We grabbed the rest of the things that I'd need to not look completely homeless. As we walked back through the store, it seemed every head turned to watch. Most people looked a little stunned to see Colt, and some were genuinely giddy about his visit to the store, in particular the two teenage girls running the checkout stands. The one whose line we ended up in nearly passed out with nerves. Her friend looked green with envy.

The cashier blushed pink under a light spray of freckles. Her hands were shaky, and I felt a little sorry for her. The most amusing part of it all was that Colt didn't even seem to notice the stir he'd caused.

He paid for my things, and the girl smiled up at him. She hadn't said a word, but her expression spoke volumes. Both young cashiers giggled wildly as we walked out.

"Is it always like that when you walk through a place?" I asked.

"Like what?"

I chuckled. "Like a damn rock star just walked through with his hair on fire. Come on, you had to notice."

"Just figured they were all staring at those beautiful tits of yours bouncing wildly in that tiny shirt." He reached up and swept his fingers across the shirt . . . and my nipple. "Nice. This braless look is working for you."

It took me a second to regain my composure. His one light touch, even through fabric, had sent a flurry of heat through my body. My profound reaction hadn't escaped his notice.

"Everything all right, darlin'?" A glimmer of a smile crossed his face as he opened the truck door for me.

I took a deep breath and climbed inside. "Everything's just fine."

EIGHT
JADE

After a quick trip to the local pharmacy to replace the birth control pills that had been lost with the backpack, something I needed so that my periods wouldn't go haywire, among other reasons, Colt drove me along the coastal highway. There was something he'd wanted to show me. Whatever it was it had him grinning like a little boy, which, for a man like him was completely inconsistent and adorable.

Jagged black rocks dotted most of the coastline, leaving only a few stretches of sand that could be used by people for fishing or surfing or whatever suited their fancy. But for the most part, the beaches were inhabited by birds. Farther out, the rocks were safe havens and rest stops for sea lions. "You've lived here your whole life?" I asked.

"Yep. My dad was a fisherman."

"So, you and your brothers are keeping up the family business?"

He nodded. "Something like that." He reached forward and switched the music.

I remembered vaguely that as I'd climbed onboard their trawler the nets looked almost pristine, as if they'd hardly been used. From the look on his face, it was obvious this wasn't a topic he wanted to discuss.

"Exactly where are you taking me?"

He turned off the highway and the truck jostled from side to side as we rolled along an unpaved road. He pulled up in front of a run-down but cool little beach cottage. Long, thin weeds covered the front yard, and they swayed in perfect unison in the ocean breeze. There were tools and ladders piled on the splintery porch lining the entire front of the house. There were patches of bald spots on the shingled roof. Two of the crust covered multi-paned windows had been replaced by brand new ones, and some of the rotted wood siding had been replaced by unpainted, new wood.

I looked over at him. "Is it yours?"

"Yeah. It'll probably take me until I'm ninety to get it fixed up, but I figure it'll be a nice place to die by then."

We climbed out of the car. The sun was beaming down on the cottage adding some sparkle to its heavily weathered facade. "It's fantastic, Colt. It looks like you're doing a great job fixing it up."

We walked up the porch steps.

"Step over those two planks," Colt said. "They're loose."

We stepped inside. The walls were covered in faded floral wallpaper that was slowly peeling away. The wood floors creaked with age as we walked into the tiny front room. There was a small pile of vintage, quaint-looking furniture piled in a corner of the space. Someone, most likely Colt, had wrapped a few sheets around the pile to protect it.

"It belonged to this really cool old lady who always smelled like cinnamon and spoke with a Scottish accent. Everyone called her Noddy, but I'm not sure why. She was a widow, and she lived out here alone. Her family almost never came to see her. I guess they were far away in Scotland or something." He walked over and picked up a plate from a box. It was one of those old fashioned hand painted porcelain plates you'd seen in an antique shop. Colt smiled weakly at the plate. "My brothers and I would come here sometimes." His voice was low as if he was thinking back to that time. "Whenever we needed to be away from my dad, we'd get on our bikes and ride over here. Noddy always had oatmeal cookies on this plate. Homemade ones too. None of that store-bought shit. It was weird. She always had them fresh baked like she knew we were coming." He put the plate down. "She knew what it was like for us. Everyone knew, but Noddy was the only one who made a point of noticing. The rest of the town was scared to death of my dad, but she wasn't. Even reported him once to child services, but we just ended up in different foster homes. As bad as we had it, it was still better when we were together." He looked around. "Never felt homesick in my life until Noddy died and they boarded up this place. After a long legal fight between her family members, it finally went on the market. By then, it had weathered away to this pile of wood, but I didn't care. I'd saved up enough to buy it."

"I'll bet Noddy would be happy to know it ended up in your care."

"Like to think so." He led me back outside, and we sat on the porch steps. "What about you? How'd you end up with that prick?"

I rarely talked about my past, but there was something about the way those pale green eyes looked at me that made me want to spill my heart out. "Never knew my mom. She left my dad when I was little. But he wasn't really a dad." I rubbed my boot over the sand on the bottom step. "He wasn't abusive or anything like that. He was just this other person living in the same apartment. He rarely paid attention to what I was doing because he just didn't care. When I was sixteen, I walked past him with a backpack full of my things. He never even looked up from the television. I walked out the door and never went back. Of course, the harsh reality of being homeless hit pretty fast. I met Ray at a burger stand. He was handsome and charming and, most importantly, he could give me shelter and food. And attention. All of a sudden I wasn't just some invisible person walking around an apartment with a dad who refused to acknowledge my existence. Ray showered me with that attention I craved. For awhile, I was convinced I loved him. Booze and drugs took away the few good traits he had."

Colt stood up and I followed.

"I've never run from Ray before," I said, "but I'm pretty sure he'll come looking for me."

Colt took my hand and led me back to the truck. "Figured that much. And I'm looking forward as hell to that day," he said darkly.

"No. The last thing I want is to cause trouble for you and your brothers. I'll stick around here long enough to make some money and then I'll move on. He'll have a harder time finding me if I keep moving."

He stopped when we got to the truck. He stepped closer. My body was wedged between him and the truck. I hadn't realized how cool the ocean breeze was until his body heat surrounded me. He reached up and pushed a strand of hair behind my ear. "So you're just going to keep moving from place to place to avoid that asshole?"

"I think that'll be best. I don't want to cause you any trouble."

There it was again, that slight smile that left a crease on the side of his mouth. "Darlin' it's too late. I've been in trouble since the second you used me as camouflage in that dark hallway."

His hand moved down along my cheek and back to my breasts. He slipped his hand under my shirt and smoothed his palm over the skin of my stomach and up to my naked breasts. I took a deep breath and swayed backward against the truck. His eyes turned that silvery gray color, that glossy shade that always seemed to appear when he was touching me, which he was doing now with every bit the same mastery as the night before.

I stood by helplessly, knowing I should be ducking away from his touch but unable to do so. I just didn't have the willpower to deny him. He was that good.

"Colt." His name came out on a ragged whisper.

"Shh, I know. I'm not going to try anything. I just want to touch you." His fingers teased and pinched my nipples into tight buds. "Is this making your pussy wet, baby?" He continued to play with my nipples, and I pushed them harder against his touch.

"Yes," I answered.

He shoved his thigh between my legs. A wide open

jeep with music blaring from its speakers rolled off onto the unpaved road leading to the cottage. A could of dust kicked up around it, but I could still see the two girls sitting in the front seat. Colt still hadn't pulled his hand from my shirt as they rolled over the long weeds and stopped in front of the house.

The girl in the passenger seat, an extremely pretty brunette dressed only in a tiny bikini, grabbed the top of the windshield and pulled herself to standing. She looked at me before turning her attention to Colt. Even then, he kept his hand under my shirt. I pulled out of his reach.

The driver turned down the music. "We thought we might find you here, Colt. Jen and I are headed to Cooper's Cove for a swim and *stuff*. You should come." She made it clear the invitation was just for Colt.

"Yeah? You know how much I like *stuff*. I might head over there in awhile."

The girl made a point of sneering at me before sitting back down. The jeep spun around and rumbled off through the same cloud of dust.

"I've got to get home," I said. "Amy is going to take me to talk to her boss, and you don't want to miss your swim," I said it briskly, as if it didn't bother me in the slightest that he was going to the beach to do *stuff* with two pretty girls. Of course, it did bother me, and I wanted to kick myself for that. It wasn't like I didn't know exactly what kind of guy Colt was, a guy who took pride in fucking a lot of girls. I needed to get that notion tucked firmly in my mind. Just like Amy and I had talked about this morning, guys like the Stone brothers were not worth the headache . . . or heartache, for that matter. And more heartache was the one damn thing I didn't need.

I climbed into the truck and barely said a word the entire ride home.

NINE
COLT

Hunter was sitting on the driveway next to his bike. He looked up over the seat of his motorcycle, and we both watched as Amy and Jade climbed into Amy's rust covered car. It was an odd, silent moment. Two brothers who had learned not to have any emotional connection to anyone and, yet, we didn't look away or say a word until the car sputtered off down the road.

Hunter turned his attention back to the bike. "Says she's got a date with some beer delivery guy or something," he said offhandedly as if he was making sure that I knew he didn't give a fuck.

"Street? Yeah, I think she'd be fighting off all sorts of guys if you weren't always lurking around like a fucking gladiator with his underwear in a bunch."

"I never tell her not to date. She can do whatever the hell she likes. Makes no fucking difference to me."

"Yeah, that's why you're holding that wrench like you're going to pound a skull with it."

He held it up and looked at me. "Maybe I've found just the skull." Hunter loved to threaten shit like that, but as kids, he'd taken the blame more than once for something I'd done just to spare me the belt. But, as we grew up and my dad became more ruthless, it was every man for himself. By that time, our mom had basically withered away from her pill addiction, an addiction made stronger by my dad's terrifying temper. It had been the first day of winter break when we lost her for good. Some kids looked forward to holidays. But for us, days off meant we were completely unprotected. My dad always made sure to leave marks in places the teachers couldn't see, but on vacations, you could get a fist to the face or a broken finger. That bleak winter day when other kids were decorating cookies with their moms, our mom crawled back into bed after shoving some frozen waffles in the toaster for us. She never got back up. Hunter plowed his fist into the headboard above her small, blue face. He was pissed as hell at her for leaving us alone.

"What's going on with you and the new girl? She's as sweet as fucking cotton candy, and Amy really likes her. Did you nail her already?"

"Nah, I think she needs some space away from asshole men for awhile."

"Right, space. Wait a minute—" He lifted his face up with a big fucking grin that I wanted to wipe off it. "Well, I'll be damned, the world is tilting off its axis, a girl said 'no' to Colt Stone."

"Shut the fuck up."

Slade's Mustang pulled into the driveway. He was on the phone as he climbed out. "We've got to make another run tomorrow," he said as he hung up.

"Again?" I asked.

"More drops mean more money," Hunter said as he sat up from under the bike.

"Yeah, and then someone gets careless and the feds catch on and then everyone is busted. More money is great, but you can't spend it if you're behind bars," I said.

Slade sat on the porch step. "I can see your point, Colt. With that face of yours, you'll be someone's *bitch* the second they lock you in."

Hunter laughed.

"A couple of fucking comedians, but you know I'm right. Rincon is getting greedy, and the more drops we make, the more people start noticing certain boats hanging out in the harbor. Then suddenly the coast guard is making note of it and then we're all wearing orange fucking coveralls. We're just the grunt guys, the middlemen, but you know we'll be the first to get hauled in."

The wrench clanged as Hunter dropped it into the tool box. "We'll drop the nets this time and do some fishing. Look, Colt, if you don't have the stomach for this, then Slade and I will go out on our own. I told you, once we have enough, we can start investing in something legit, like flipping real estate or a mechanic shop. We just need enough laundered capital to move us to the next level. Unless you've got some other brilliant way for us to make some cash, apart from you selling that face of yours on a street corner."

Now it was Slade's turn to laugh.

"Fuck off. I'm still with you. I'm just stating the obvious."

Hunter got up and wiped the grease from his hands on a rag that had just as much black grease on it. "What's eating you, Colt? You're not usually like this. That pretty stray kitten got your balls in a knot? Maybe you're thinking about the girl and a happy ending in your little cottage."

I pulled out a joint and lit it. "Yep, that's it. You know me and my fairy tale dreams. Not that any of that sounds too bad. I mean, beats ending up six feet under with a Styrofoam headstone that you guys scratch my name on with a fucking permanent marker."

Slade looked over at Hunter. "Guess he's right. It

would have to be a permanent marker. That other shit would just get washed away in the rain."

"Nothing wrong with pencil," Hunter said with a shrug. His face smoothed, and he looked at me. "We'll get there, Colt. Slade and I don't like this kind of work either, but it's making us money fast. Just keep those balls wrapped in steel. Unless of course they're wrapped in that little stowaway's plump pink lips. Man, she is something. No wonder that jerk was going out of his way to keep her."

Slade hopped off the steps. "That's what I was going to tell you. When we were done fishing this morning, we stopped to refuel at the dock near Bootlegger's. Overheard some guys, who were in Bootlegger's when we were ripping those assholes to pieces, talking. That fool, Ray Ward, or whatever the hell her sugar daddy's name is, he's pissed as hell that his guys got their asses beat."

Hunter smiled. "I'll bet."

"No, I mean he was pissed at them. Fired their asses and sent them on their way crying and sucking their thumbs. Now a pansy like that isn't going to walk around long without a team of thugs to cover his primped and powdered ass. He's hiring another crew." Slade looked over at me. "You better keep a close eye on that special piece of cake cuz he's going to come looking for her. I'm sure of it."

Just thinking about the fucker having his hands on

Jade made my pulse speed up. "Hope he does come after her. I'm ready for some one on one time with him." I headed toward the truck.

"Where are you going in your swim trunks?" Slade asked.

"Jen and Tina are going out to the cove to swim."

"Wait for me to change," Slade called. "I'm bored."

I raised my middle finger to him. "Find your own fucking threesome. We pretty faced boys don't like to share our spoils." I slammed the door to the truck. I hadn't really planned on going to the cove. But when I realized that Jade was the reason behind me not being in the mood, I knew I had to go. I hadn't stopped thinking about her since I'd had her up against that wall in the utility closet. And the last thing I needed was a girl I couldn't stop thinking about. An afternoon with Jen and Tina was a sure cure for a stiff cock, and mine had been aching since I woke up with my sea salt kitten stretched out next to me.

TEN
JADE

Amy had gotten a fifty dollar tip from a stuffy-looking man in a navy blue suit and wonky toupee. She was amped up about it, and I was excited for her. She was the type of person you wanted to cheer for no matter what she was up to. And since she'd put her own neck on the line to get me a two week trial at the job, I was determined not to let her down. I had no experience waiting tables, but her boss, Jack, a leathery old, ex-military guy who was half teddy bear, half grenade with the pin pulled, decided I would look good in the unofficial bar uniform, an undersized mini-skirt and a blouse that had to be tied up right beneath my bra. Buttons, he noted, had to be undone at least halfway down my cleavage. Amy enthusiastically pointed out that at least we weren't topless and that showing leg and cleavage always brought better tips. I was put on dishwashing and other menial tasks for the first week, and if I didn't break too many glasses, I would get to try serving. Even with long rubber gloves, my hands were raw and my back hurt from bending over the giant dishwashing sink. But it had felt good to work and earn my own money. I was sure the job would get easier.

The coastal fog had rolled in, but it was light and frilly, not the usual layer of soup. Amy's car made plenty of unhealthy noises, but she just ignored them.

"Hey, tomorrow I'll take you to pick a cute blouse at the thrift store. I get a lot of my work clothes there." Amy said as she cranked the music in her car. "My treat."

"Amy, you've already done so much for me. Jack said if things work out, I can rent that little room behind the bar from him. He'll just charge me fifty dollars a month. And without a car, living at the job will be very convenient."

She crinkled her little nose. "I don't know if that's such a good idea, Jade. As you might have noticed, Lazy Daze is in a really shitty part of town. You're a lot safer with Colt."

"I can't leech off of them for long. I really need to be independent for a change. When I ran away from home, I'd never thought anything through, and I had no chance to make it on my own. Now I've run again, but this time I'm determined to survive without any help."

"At least stick it out here until you have enough money to get a decent place. I was serious about us getting a place together some time. It would be fun."

"I agree. I guess I'll see how it goes. It's really nice of the brothers to let me stay, but it's kind of—"

"Awkward?" she finished for me. "Colt's a guy who can sweep in and tear a girl's heart apart and not even notice he's done it. But if you keep your head on straight and don't let him get to you, it'll be fine."

I smiled thinking about how quickly she'd let Hunter carry her into the bedroom this morning.

Amy pulled up into her own driveway, and we climbed out. She looked toward her house. It was pitch dark. "You'd think she could leave the damn light on for me." It was the first time I'd heard her sound angry. "It's like having my very own middle-aged kid. And, frankly, I'm getting kind of tired of being the only adult in the house."

"Anytime you need me to keep an eye on her, let me know. You've done so much for me, and I really want to be able to return the favor."

She leaned over and hugged me. "Just having you around is the favor. The only other people I have to talk to are the pigs in that house next door, my delusional mother and Jack. You're a breath of fresh, minty air."

I smiled. "Glad to be minty then. Good night." I turned toward the house. "Crap, looks like no one's up. I don't have a key."

Amy waved her hand toward the house. "Don't think they ever bother to lock it. No one in this town is stupid or desperate enough to break into *that* house."

"Makes sense." I walked across Amy's non-existent front lawn to the house. I climbed the rickety porch steps. The knob turned. There was a light on in the hallway and someone had left the television on, but it was muted. The couch was empty. I could use it as a bed.

I walked into the kitchen. Magically, the sink was once again filled with dirty dishes. Somehow, I wasn't surprised. I tiptoed down the hallway, but the creaky wood floor made noises anyhow. As I turned to slip into the bathroom, I heard a noise coming from Colt's room. I decided to stop in his room first and tell him about the job. I pushed open the door. The yellow light from the hallway flowed into his small room. Colt was stretched out naked on his bed. One of the girls from the jeep, also naked, was sleeping between his legs with her head on Colt's thigh and her face nearly nestled against his cock. The second girl, wearing only a bra, was fast asleep with her arm draped over Colt's chest. None of it should have shocked me, and yet, I was shocked. None of it should have bothered me, and yet, I was bothered. And this was why I needed to get out of this house soon. As I backed out, the floorboards creaked and Colt's eyes flickered open. Our gazes stuck for a second before I managed to make my escape. I went into the bathroom and shut the door.

I turned on the water to wash my face. My refection stared back at me with pink blushed cheeks and a hurt expression. I was pissed at myself for feeling that way. I knew exactly what kind of guy Colt was. For fucksake he was participating in a damn contest and I was number fifty-something. Why I'd imagined anything different than the naked man stretched out between two naked girls was almost comical. Colt was *that guy*, the one who plowed through life leaving nothing but broken hearts behind and not giving a shit about the flood of tears in his wake. He certainly didn't need me to add my tears to the mix. I just needed to get on my feet and get the hell out of here.

The cool water felt good as I cupped it in my palms and pressed it against my face. Colt had generously bought me my bathroom essentials, including my favorite citrus smelling face wash. Contrary to what I'd just seen in the bedroom and those few unguarded moments in the utility closet when my flustered state had succumbed to his charm, his handsome face and his amazing fingers, Colt had behaved as a gentleman. Far kinder than any of the men I'd hung around in my recent past. And the cottage he'd shown me with so much pride glinting in his green eyes had made him that much better. That might have been the whole problem. I'd already built him up to be someone he wasn't.

Cool air brushed my legs as the bathroom door opened. I reached blindly around for a towel, realizing I hadn't even thought about one until now. A towel brushed my hand. I grabbed it and wiped my face. At least he'd taken the time to pull on his boxers.

Colt leaned against the bathroom sink and looked at me. He was a big guy for such a small bathroom, but he was the kind of man who would have a huge presence even in a massive ballroom. His shoulders nearly spanned the bathroom vanity. Black ink swirled in every direction on his arms and chest. The mosaic of tattoos vibrated with each movement. Then, in the mirror, I caught his reflection. His back was turned toward the glass. The scars outnumbered the tattoos. Thin, brutal strap marks crisscrossed the tanned skin giving weight to the horror story of his childhood.

He caught me staring at the reflection but ignored my expression. He was definitely not the type of guy who wanted to be pitied. Far from it.

"Street texted me earlier that you got the job," he started in on casual conversation as if I hadn't just seen him in bed with two girls. I supposed that scenario was as common to him as the tide pulling back from the sand at dawn.

"A trial basis," I said, continuing with my bedtime routine. I pressed some toothpaste on the toothbrush. "I should be able to pay you back for all this soon. Then I'll be out of your way. Jack, my boss, has a room for rent."

"Jade, you can't live in that cave room behind the bar. It's not safe."

"I'll be fine. I'll get a really mean cat or something." I couldn't hide the disappointment in my voice. It was stupid because there was nothing between us. I'd even turned him down this morning, but I was hurt. For some ridiculous reason, I thought he'd hold off on his contest pursuits until I was out of the house. Now I saw how stupid that was. He stepped closer. I could smell girl's perfume on his skin. It made me step away.

I shoved the brush into my mouth to let him know I was done talking. He didn't move. He just stared at me with those eyes that were a jade green under the bathroom light. I spit out the foam and clumsily wiped my mouth. He had me completely flustered.

"I'll bunk on the couch, of course. I'll keep out of the way, I promise." The discussion of sleeping arrangements had never been approached. Even though I'd never felt pangs of homesickness in my life, I did long for my comfortable bed in Ray's house. Of course, it was only comfortable when the man wasn't in it.

He reached up to my face. I held my breath in expectation. "You missed some," he said as his rough thumb wiped away excess toothpaste.

He lowered his hand and leaned closer. "You can breathe now, darlin', I'm leaving." He walked out.

My shoulders sank as I released the air that had been jammed in my lungs. I stood with my hands braced against the counter staring down into the moldy sink. Once again, I'd fled my life without giving any thought to my future. I was sure that Jack wouldn't rent the room to me until he knew I was a good fit for his bar. Not that I had one penny to give him yet. I would sleep on the couch and try to be invisible for a few weeks. Colt's brief visit in the bathroom had left me completely shaken and my heart pounding. A guy like him was the last thing I needed now. A guy like Colt Stone was the last thing I ever needed.

ELEVEN
COLT

Our boat, the *Durango*, sliced through the emerald green water. I had that creepy feeling you get on the back of your neck when you know something is off. I'd had the same feeling that morning my mom had crawled into bed for the last time. I'd finished smearing peanut butter on my half of the burned waffle, and as I screwed the cap back on the peanut butter, a shiver went through me as if an icy wind had blown through the house. I went through the rest of the morning with an uneasy feeling, thinking something wasn't quite right. And I remember thinking I should go in and see what Mom was doing, but I stopped myself. Something told me not to go down the hallway to her bedroom. It was Hunter who finally got hungry for some lunch and who had plodded down the hallway to her room. I knew, for some weird reason, I knew.

Our connection, the boat sent to pick up the drugs, was moored at the precise coordinates they'd sent us earlier that morning. The sky was clear blue, and the sun was strumming a solid beat on the deck of the *Durango*. My dad had named the boat after his hometown. We'd never changed it. He'd be turning in his grave if he knew his pride and joy, the boat he'd loved far more than his sons and wife, the boat he'd never raised a cruel hand to, was hauling cocaine across the Pacific. That thought always made me smile. Anything we might do to piss our dad off in his eternal sleep was fine by me. We'd lived in hell while he was alive. It would be fitting to know that he was living in it now.

Hunter lowered the spyglass. "Rincon said they've got a new guy in charge. Worked with some of the cartels south of the border, a real motherfucker."

I leaned against the railing. "Great. This gig just keeps getting better."

Slade steered toward them and shut down the boat's engine fifty yards away from our connection. Hunter walked along the starboard side with his spyglass. There was nothing for miles but deep blue ocean, which was what we wanted and needed. I always breathed a sigh of relief when our highly valuable and highly illegal cargo was out of our hands and in theirs. I had no idea where it went after it was carried out of our cargo hold, and I didn't really give a fuck as long as we got the cash for making the drop. Our part of the job brought the least headaches with it, except we had to trust that both sides had dependable people working for them. If word got out, we'd be targets, not only for the feds, but for pirates or thieves looking to make a nice score on a cargo hold full of blow.

The other boat lowered a dinghy into the water. Their man stayed on watch from the crow's nest while Hunter kept a lookout from the stern. Three men climbed into the small boat. Two I recognized as the usual goons who picked up the cargo. The third was a small guy with a shaved head, black beard and mustache. He had a shoulder holster on over his army green t-shirt. Nothing about him looked friendly.

They glided over the waves in the dinghy. As they reached the *Durango*, I threw down the rope ladder. They tied off the boat and climbed aboard. The new guy had beady dark eyes. He glanced around with amusement at our rusty trawler.

"Who's in charge here?" he asked.

Hunter stepped around with his spyglass. "I am. Why do you ask?"

The man stared up at my brother who outweighed him by a good fifty pounds. That seemed to amuse him, too, either that or the arrogant smirk was just part of his natural expression. "I always like to ask so I know who to direct the conversation to," he said. He looked at me. "Just you two? I also like to know how many people are onboard when I step onto a boat deck. You understand."

Hunter pointed up to the pilot house. "One more guy. He's in the captain's chair."

The man squinted up to the pilot house. "Wave him down here. I like all hands on deck while we check the load."

Hunter stared at him a second, and I wondered if he would challenge the guy's orders. Then he waved up at Slade to come down. We always kept pistols tucked under our shirts, but we'd never had to pull them out. Today my hand was itching to touch mine. It was obvious that Hunter had the same urge as me.

Slade came down from the pilot house looking the way Hunter and I were feeling, tense. The two usual goobers who accompanied these pickups looked just as uneasy with their new boss.

The man looked around with his shifty, deep set eyes as if he was expecting a bunch of armed men to jump out from behind the nets. "This is it then?" he asked after giving the deck a brief once over.

"Just us, man. Let's get this going. We don't usually stand here for a fucking tea party." Hunter was on his last nerve.

The guy glared at him in a short contest of chicken

to see if Hunter would look away. No fucking way that Hunter would do that. Impatience and a strong desire to get these assholes and this shit off the boat, prodded me toward the cargo hold. Shifty-eyed man followed.

I opened the trap door. The cold barrel of the man's gun pressed hard against my temple. The sound of him cocking his gun rattled in my ear.

"What the fuck are you doing?" Hunter asked between gritted teeth, now having no choice except to control his temper. Otherwise, my brains were going to be splattered all over my dad's precious boat.

"Assurance," the guy sneered in my ear. He motioned for the other two to climb into the hold and haul the stuff up. The blow was in plastic bags, which had then been wrapped in brown paper and tied into manageable bundles, bundles that could easily be thrown overboard if needed.

Hunter and Slade both looked as if fire would shoot from their nostrils if they took a breath. Instead, they held in the rage and waited while the men dragged up the bundles and counted them. The jerk with the gun against my head reached down and pulled a knife from his leather holster. He sliced one bundle of the coke and dipped his finger in it. He rubbed it across his gums. "Lucky for you, it's good stuff," he snarled at the side of my face. "Get this to the dinghy."

His two coworkers worked quickly to get the

bundles down to their boat. The guy shoved the barrel harder against my temple and gave it a little turn to twist my skin painfully.

He leaned closer. "I've got to compliment you. You didn't flinch once while I had this Glock pushed up against your skull." He lowered his gun and put it in the holster. "I've had men piss their pants when I shoved a gun against their head, but you just stood there cool as a fucking cucumber. Impressive." With that, he walked to the stern and disappeared over the railing.

I looked at my brothers. Hunter's knuckles were white as he unfurled his fists.

The dinghy motor buzzed like a hive of angry bees as they returned to their boat. Slade shook his head as he climbed back up to the pilot house. "Don't know about you two, but I'm ready to get the fuck out of here."

Hunter didn't say a word. He walked back to the railing and lifted his spyglass to his eye.

TWELVE
JADE

Susan, the woman who usually served drinks with Amy, couldn't get her car started. Jack tossed me an apron and a tray and told me to just follow what Amy was doing. I was nervous as heck at first. I was sure I would spill everyone's drinks, but the customers weren't the spoiled, whiny type like some of Ray's snooty friends. Everyone was kickback and not terribly demanding. They knew I was in training. They were a rowdy, loud and hard drinking bunch just out to have a good time. My bad case of nerves eventually dissolved.

After a few hours, I found myself enjoying the work, and the tips were a nice addition. Susan's misfortune had made it my lucky night. Jack seemed to take notice that I was handling the server job without too much trouble. I hoped that meant I'd be off dishwashing soon.

One table, a booth near the bar, was filled with four fishermen who'd come in from a long day on the water. They smelled of salt and fish and sweat, but they ordered a lot of drinks and they tipped well, so it was easy to put up with their *manly* aroma. I placed their fourth pitcher of beer on the table. The beers were finally catching up to them.

The one who they called Bobby lifted a wavering finger at me. "You'd make a very pretty mermaid with that silvery-white hair." His words were slow and stretched out from the beer.

"Thank you. But I'm not sure how successful I'd be without a fish tail."

Their laughter vibrated the table in the booth. I spun around to head back to the bar for some more drinks just as Hunter walked inside. The serious flood of nerves I'd been dealing with when I first started waiting tables returned ten-fold when Colt walked in behind him. As if there had been some weird magnetic field between us, Colt's green gaze instantly found mine. We stared at each other as if stuck together. I broke away first and returned to the bar.

Amy was behind the counter filling a pitcher of beer. Her eyes were glued to Hunter as he made his way across the room. Chairs scraped the floor as all three brothers sat down at one of my tables.

I shot Amy an anxious look, and she read my mind.

"I'll wait on them. You can take my table over by the window. But I've got to warn you, they're kind of obnoxious. I've never seen them before. Apparently, they're just passing through. Thank god."

I looked over at the window table. There were three guys wearing leather motorcycle jackets and smug expressions. One had shaved blond hair and a jaw and forehead that reminded me of Frankenstein. He caught me looking over at them and winked. I looked quickly away. "You're right, they look obnoxious. But I'll still trade with you." I lifted some glasses from the shelves under the counter. Amy, who never missed a damn thing, saw that my hand was shaking.

She took the glass from my fingers and placed it on the tray. "You need to tell yourself that it's just Colt. He may not look it, but he's just a mere mortal who happens to look like a fucking Adonis, and, unfortunately, he's just as smooth as a Greek god too. But he's just a man. Now take a deep breath."

I stopped and pulled in a long, slow breath, then released it. Amy's eyes widened at someone behind me. I looked at her. She winked, assuring me that it was Colt.

I turned around. His smile immediately sent the usual flurry of butterflies bouncing around in my stomach. "They've got you waiting tables, huh?"

"Susan had car problems. I'll be back on dishes tomorrow, but I don't mind."

"How was the fishing?" I asked. They'd left early in the morning, and I had been relieved to have the house to myself for a few hours. I'd had a chance to reflect on everything that had happened in the last few days. The peace and solitude had felt like a long, luxurious soak in a bubble bath.

Colt combed his fingers back through his hair. "Fishing wasn't the best, but we all made it back." He, of course, didn't have the same semi-rank odor of the other fishermen I'd just served beer to. I'd already figured that fishing wasn't really their thing, but it was none of my business. What I did know was that I certainly didn't need to get tangled up with another guy who was always one step away from jail. Of course, I could have been jumping to conclusions. The three brothers could have been up to something completely legitimate out there on the water. But they didn't exactly look or act like choir boys. The complete opposite, in fact. I probably wasn't jumping too far.

"Are you waiting on our table?" Colt asked. "We need a pitcher and some tequila shots too."

"Yeah, yeah," Amy said from behind the counter. "Keep your panties on. I'll get it to you in a second."

I tried to scoot past him, but he blocked me. It was only for a brief moment, but it felt as if hot static charges flew back and forth between us. I didn't have the courage to even look up at him. It was always best to avoid his face, those green eyes, that cool, calm exterior that made me a trembling mess inside. He finally stepped back. His fingers brushed my arm as I slipped past him. I felt his light touch all the way across the floor as if his fingers had seared my skin.

The only way I was going to survive the rest of the work shift was by completely ignoring his presence. I was never the type of girl to fall into a nervous muddle about a guy. I couldn't understand why Colt had me so distracted. Right from the start, in the utility closet, the way I'd immediately succumbed to him when he pressed his hand between my legs, it was as if he'd cast me under his spell. But I needed to break myself free of it, and fast.

I'd been avoiding the table by the window, but the big dude with the square head had waved Amy over. I walked toward him. "Hi, I'm Jade, and I'll be your server for the rest of the night." I glanced down at their beer bottles. "Another round?"

One of the men had a nasty scar running across his cheek. He had thin lips that he kept licking with the tip of his tongue, reminding me of a snake. He looked pointedly at my breasts. "The other girl had more buttons undone," he said. "Don't think we'll be tipping you as well unless you show a little more cleavage."

I ignored the comment. "I'll bring you another round." I leaned over to pick up the beer bottles.

The square faced man leaned over to make a point of looking at my legs. "Those are some nice panties under that teeny skirt." I straightened, again ignoring the comment and reminding myself that they were drunk. I knew, too well, how awful some people could be when they'd had too much alcohol.

They whistled loudly as I walked back across to the bar. As hard as I'd tried to ignore him, my eyes flicked in Colt's direction. He was sitting up straight staring hard at the three jerks at the window table. The evening had been going so well, but it was disintegrating fast. There were still two hours before closing, and with the way the beer was flowing, the place would be filled with drunks long before the doors were locked. I just had to keep my wits about me.

Just as I had that thought, four women walked into the place. The second they spotted the Stone brothers, they headed their direction. Two of them pulled up chairs, one of them climbed onto Slade's lap and wrapped her arms around his neck before kissing him. The fourth, a curvy girl with long, dark hair and cherry red lips climbed onto Colt's lap. His arm went around her, blowing apart my fleeting fantasy that he would push her away instead.

Amy came over to grab some limes and salt. "I really

hate those girls. We went to school with them. Two of them just got back home from college for summer break. The one sitting next to Hunter—"

"You mean the one who was decent enough to pull up a chair instead of a lap?"

"Yeah, she's not quite as forward as her two giggly friends, but she's sly. She's going to some school on the east coast. Her family owns that big house that sits up on the hill overlooking the bay. She's always had a big thing for Hunter. Naturally, her father would never approve, but she still likes to follow him around like a lost puppy." Amy looked upset and that was rare for her.

I touched her arm as she picked up her tray. "And she's got nothing on you, Amy. Really."

She shook her head. "Doesn't matter. She can have him. He's nothing but trouble anyhow." She carried off her tray.

Reluctantly, I delivered the beers over to the three creepy customers. Now that the women had joined the Stone brothers, I was exceptionally glad not to have their table. I could put up with a few rude comments and lascivious tongue movements if it meant not having to wait on Colt while some girl was wrapped around him.

I forced a polite smile as I placed the beers down on the table. The three men sat silently and watched me. I was just about to make a clean escape with my tray, but as I turned, the man with the scar leaned over and grabbed my ass.

The only thing I'd heard was a shocked female gasp and a chair scraping the ground. A stunned silence followed. I hadn't seen him grab the guy. Hell, I hadn't even seen him move across the room. Colt had the man who'd grabbed me in his grasp. Then, in one fluid movement, he threw the man against the wall. His friends flew out of the booth and lunged at Colt, but Hunter and Slade, who had raced over too, made a wall with their bodies.

Jack came out of his office with a sawed off baseball bat. "Damnit, Colt, you're going to pay if there's any damage."

"No damage, Jack. Just this asshole's face, but considering how fucking ugly—" Colt raised his fist to hit the man.

"No!" I yelled. "Stop, Colt. What the hell are you doing?"

He looked at me. It seemed he'd almost surprised himself with his actions.

"Let him go." I broke into sobs and raced out the door.

I had no place to run. I had nothing. I had no car, no home, no family. Staying with Ray would have been like staying in hell, but now that I'd stepped out into the world, the reality of my bleak situation was smacking me hard. I leaned against the back of Amy's car and covered my face to cry.

Footsteps crunched the gravel in the parking lot. I lifted my face from my hands. Colt stood nearby, looking dangerous and confused and a little less angry than a few seconds before.

"That little testosterone exhibition will get me fired, and I really needed that job." A laugh popped from my mouth. "I ran out here and realized I didn't even have a fucking car to hide in. I've got nothing, and now I'll be out of a job."

"I'll talk to Jack. He won't fire you. I'm sorry, Jade. I saw that guy grab you and— I'm sorry." He turned around and took three steps, then stopped. "No. You know what? Fuck it." He strode toward me. I gasped as he grabbed my arms. "I'm not fucking sorry." His mouth slammed down over mine. The kiss was punishing, hard, hungry and I wanted more. My lips parted farther, and his kiss deepened, making my knees weaken to butter.

I was nearly breathless when he lifted his mouth from mine. His eyes were vivid green as he gazed down at me. "Seeing that guy touch you was too much. I couldn't stop myself. Before I knew it, I was flying across that bar thinking, he touched you and I was going to have to pound him for it. No one fucking touches you except me." His mouth came down over mine again. He held me so tightly, I was sure he'd squeeze the breath from me. "Since I had you pressed up against the wall in that closet, I knew that you had to be mine," he whispered against my mouth.

My mind was a hurricane of emotions, but his last words were like a fist to my chest. I stepped back and pulled away from his arms. The last thing I needed was to be another man's possession. Even a man as heartbreaking as Colt.

He stared at me with a look of hurt as if now he'd taken a fist to the chest. I wiped my tears away and took a breath. If I had any chance at independence, I was going to have to stop crying like a little girl. I walked past him, leaving him standing in the parking lot as I returned to my job.

THIRTEEN
COLT

I stared up at the stains on my ceiling where rainwater had seeped in through the shabby roof and soaked the attic. It had been a shitty fucking day, starting with a gun to my head and ending with a major slap to my ego. I'd shocked the hell out of myself with my reaction in the bar. The second that jerk's hand flew to Jade's ass, I'd exploded with rage. I'd come to Amy's rescue more than once when someone had been rude to her. Although most local guys knew not to bother her because Hunter would tear them to shreds. But this had been different. This had been an overwhelming urge to pound someone for getting near Jade. I had no apology for what I'd done because I was damn sure I'd do it again.

It was the last thing I ever wanted, to feel this way

about someone. Attachments like this were only followed by heartbreak, and I wasn't into heartbreak. I wasn't into fucking attachments. Jade was determined to get out on her own as soon as possible, and it seemed that was for the best. Just as I had that thought, there was a tiny knock at the door.

She opened it without me answering. Jade stepped into the room wearing the t-shirt she'd borrowed from me to sleep in. The thought of her naked body under my t-shirt was so erotic, she might as well have whispered the words, 'fuck me' in my ear. I sat up and swung my legs over the bed. She looked small and lost and sad standing in the middle of my room, but I fought the urge to pull her into my arms.

Her lips parted to speak, but it took her a second to get the words out. "So, I'm laying out there on your lumpy couch thinking about stuff. First of all, it's really lonely and quiet out there, and I kept hearing this crinkling sound under my head. Someone had shoved a half-eaten bag of potato chips under the cushion. Who does that?"

I wasn't completely sure where this was going, but she was talking to me and that was all that mattered. "Probably Slade, he wears the slob crown around here."

"Not that, well yeah, that's definitely a slob thing. I mean who wastes a perfectly good bag of potato chips?"

I smiled and still fought the urge to walk across the room and grab her.

Her face smoothed, the smile faded and she crossed her arms over herself. She took a breath. "The thing is, Colt, I don't want to be owned." Her soft words drifted around the room. "I've been there, and I don't like it."

I stood up. She gazed at my naked body. My cock had been hard since she'd walked into the room. I stopped just a few feet from her. She lifted her eyes to my face.

"That guy touched you tonight and something snapped deep in my chest. I don't know anything about love, Jade. I grew up with fear, pain and every other emotion, but love wasn't part of it. All I know is the instinct to protect. My brothers and I learned early on to protect each other and our mom, but I never thought of it as love. It was just this instinctual part of me that knew there were certain people that I would protect with my fucking life. Amy is part of that circle, but I've never felt that way about any other woman until I met you. When I held you in that foil blanket on the boat that night, all I could think was— just let that fucking douche try to come near her again. He wouldn't have a chance against me. I'd rip him to fucking pieces. So, I'm sorry if my attempt at showing that I care about you is a little—"

"Primitive?" she asked with a faint smile.

I scrubbed my hair back with my fingers. "Yeah, primitive. It's the only way I know to show someone that they mean something to me."

She smiled again, but this time it was a flirty one. Her mood had lightened. She stepped closer to just within my reach. "I'll bet you can think of some other ways to show it if you give it a little thought." She reached down, took hold of the hem of the t-shirt and inched it up to expose her panties. Then she stopped. My breath stopped with it.

She let the hem slide down her sleek thighs again. "See, here's the thing. It sucks having to confess this, but I haven't stopped thinking about the first time we kissed, the first time you touched me. We were complete strangers, but my body reacted as if it was no longer being controlled by my mind. I rather liked it. Actually, I fucking loved it. It was like you cast this amazing spell over me, a spell to forget everything that was dark and ugly. I think that's what I need now. A magic spell. No thinking. No worrying about relationships or emotions or being someone's possession. I just want to feel that same physical ecstasy you showed me on that first night. No heartstrings attached."

"I can do no heartstrings. In fact, I'm a pro at it. And as for the magic . . . " I reached for her, but she held up a hand to stop me.

"One rule, though, and this might change your

mind. The contest is over. From this point on, until we both grow tired of each other, I'm your only *contestant*."

I paused as if I was thinking it over. But I really wasn't. It was an easy decision. "If that's your only rule, then it's a deal."

She stuck her hand out to shake on it, but I didn't take it. "I've got a rule of my own. And as far as I'm concerned, it's non-negotiable. I always use a condom."

She smiled.

"I know that sounds comical to you, but I'd rather use a shield than suffer the consequences."

"I think that's a good rule."

"Nope, you haven't let me finish." I moved closer. Her breasts lifted and fell with each breath. With every movement, her taut nipples pressed against the thin cotton fabric of the shirt. "I'm just letting you know that I'm clean. I know you're on birth control. I want you unfiltered."

She laughed at my odd use of the term.

"Are you laughing at me, darlin'?" I pulled her into my arms.

"You just made me sound like a bottle of apple juice."

"Did I? Well, good, because I plan to drink every last drop." I kissed her lightly on the mouth. "When I'm inside of you, which I plan to be . . . often . . . I want to feel all of you. I don't want any latex barrier. I just want your hot pussy around me and nothing else." My words made her shudder in my arms. I lowered my mouth to her ear. "What do you say to my rule?"

"I guess if it's non-negotiable, there's not much to say," she said breathlessly. She curled her hand around the back of my neck and my hands swept under the t-shirt. As her lips parted, my cock pressed against her stomach, asking urgently for attention. She lowered one hand between us and took hold of me, rubbing her thumb teasingly over the moist, fleshy tip.

I groaned against her mouth. "Sorry, darlin', been waiting too long." I lifted her up and walked the three steps to the wall. I pushed her up against it, kissing her hard and without any thought to what I was doing. All I knew was I needed to be inside of her.

She planted her feet on the floor long enough to shove off her panties. "Yes, Colt, yes please."

I didn't need the polite invitation. It was going to take a bullet to my head to stop me at this point. She wrapped her arms around my neck. I braced her against the wall as her long legs went around me. I looked down at the space between us. I wanted to watch my cock drive into her, into the wet pussy that so sweetly beckoned me to fuck it.

I shoved the t-shirt up above her tits and stared down at her waiting pussy. "God, you're beautiful, Jade." I pressed the tip of my cock against her tight hole.

It was wet with cream, waiting anxiously for more of me. I drove into her. She tangled her fingers in my hair. Her head lulled back against the wall, and she moaned appreciatively as I impaled her again and again.

My hand went under her ass. I held her against me using the wall behind her as resistance. She clung tightly to me with her arms and legs. I reached between our bodies and pressed my thumb against her clit. She immediately took it as an invite to grind against my finger. Her legs clamped tightly around me, and she tightened her ass to meet each of my thrusts. We were in perfect rhythm. My bedroom wall shook as if an earthquake had struck the house.

"I won't fucking stop until you come, baby. I can stay hard all night for you."

Hot moisture coated my thumb as she pushed her clit against it. She rocked against me, clenching her pussy tight around my throbbing cock. It took all my will not to finish. Her fingers pulled my hair. "Harder," she pleaded.

I slammed my hips forward, pushing deeper each time. Her eyes drifted shut, and her head leaned back against the wall." Fuck yes, Colt," she cried as her pussy clenched tightly around me.

As she melted softer in my arms, I lifted my hand from her clit and held her in my iron grasp. I ground into her, pushing tiny mewls of pleasure from her pink lips, the sound of which brought me over the edge. I clutched her tightly and spilled my hot seed inside of her.

Her legs dropped to the floor, and she collapsed into my arms. A thunderous round of applause rolled up the hallway. "About fucking time you two!" Slade yelled.

"Could cut the tension between you with a fucking machete," Hunter followed.

A dark pink blush rose in Jade's cheeks as she pressed her face against me. "Were we that loud?" she asked. "Or maybe I should ask was it that obvious— the tension, I mean?"

I lifted her up into my arms and carried her to the bed. "To the first question," I said, "might just have left a few cracks in the plaster, so yes. To the second question . . . yes."

FOURTEEN
JADE

It was that weird twilight time in the morning when the room was still gray enough that sleep beckoned you to stay tucked in bed. Which was easier than ever this morning. I'd slept solidly for the first time in months, as long as I didn't count the two times Colt had woken me. Those luxurious interruptions had only added to the fulfilling night of sleep.

I had no idea exactly when it had struck me that I wanted this, just something deliciously physical to fill the giant void that seemed to be my life at the moment. But I was fairly certain the notion had taken hold right after I'd walked away from Colt in the parking lot. The three obnoxious guys had decided to move on, and I continued waiting tables, hoping Jack would ignore what had happened. Colt had come back in, and I'd tried my hardest to ignore him. But ignoring Colt Stone was like trying not to notice a category five hurricane. Impossible. He just had a huge presence, as if fireworks were always following him and going off in a bright, loud display with every step. He'd headed straight over to Jack, and they talked for a few minutes. The softer, gentler Jack had returned. His big meaty face could change expression from angry and harsh to kind and smiling in a flash. Whatever Colt had told him seemed to have worked. Jack hadn't fired me. The Stone brothers had left a few minutes after that. And as I'd watched Colt walk out, I realized how badly I wanted to be in those strong, protective arms. I'd kept up a strong front by walking away from him in the parking lot, but the truth was, inside I had been crumpling with a need to be held by him.

My mind debate had continued in the darkness of their shabby little family room with only the lumpy couch and potato chip bag beneath me. That was when I'd come up with the idea that I could be just like these men. Enjoying physical pleasures and avoiding anything emotional.

Colt stretched his muscular legs out beneath the blanket and turned to face me. Long black lashes still shaded his cheeks, and a soft snore followed. He was even breathtaking fast asleep. The plan was perfect except one major flaw— avoiding emotional attachments to a man like Colt was going to take a will of iron.

I stared at him in the pale light pouring into the room through the worn drapes. He was sleeping soundly. I reached under the covers and ran my fingertips down his rock hard abdomen to the crisp black line of hair that led down to his cock.

He groaned but didn't open his eyes. "Are you taking advantage of me while I'm asleep?" he asked groggily.

"I doubt it's possible to take advantage of a man like you but, yes, that's what I'm attempting." I wrapped my fingers around his now hardened cock. "Is it working?"

"I'm completely yours. I only ask that you treat me gently."

I laughed. "No promises." I gave his shoulder a shove, and he rolled onto his back. I straddled him and gazed down at the incredibly hot man between my legs. A slight breath of disbelief lodged in my throat. He was so extraordinary, I needed to convince myself that I hadn't just conjured him in my imagination. His talent in bed was just as breathtaking as the man himself. I'd mentioned casually, in passing, that once we tired of each other we would go our separate ways. I just wondered how on earth I'd ever get bored of him. No doubt, he would tire of me much faster. That thought dampened my spirits some.

He reached up and pressed his hand against my face. I pushed my cheek harder against his palm. More than once during our long moments of passion, he had done something similar, like a caress on my cheek or a kiss on my shoulder. Each time had made my throat tighten at the notion that there might be more to all this than really great sex. But I needed to ignore those crazy thoughts.

"You look just as beautiful this morning as you did last night when you came scooting into my room wearing my t-shirt."

"Since I have mussed up pillow hair and puffy eyes, I know you're only saying that to have your way with me. Which is a waste of time—" I reached between my legs and shifted the tip of his cock beneath me. "Because I'm pretty damn sure that you're going to have your way with me." I slid down over him.

His green eyes darkened to a muted greenish-gray color as he watched me lower myself onto his cock.

I rubbed my hands over his hard chest. "Or maybe it'll be the other way around." My words were coming out between breaths.

His hips lifted to meet me as my pussy swallowed the thick, hard length of him.

"God, baby," Colt grunted. "You're so tight, I just want to stay inside of you all fucking day."

I braced my hands on each side of him. He gripped

my hips and held me over him as I rose up and then lowered myself down over him again. Each time, he filled me deeper and more completely, and each time, I felt more connected to the man. This was all supposed to be physical. It was going to be harder than I'd thought keeping my heart out of it. I was sure for him it was purely sex. I needed to think of it the same way.

Colt reached around and held my ass tightly as he ground himself into me. My head spun as every movement brought me closer to climax. "Your pussy is so damn sweet, I don't want anyone else to ever touch it but me. Do you fucking hear me?" he groaned. "It belongs to me. I can't get enough of it. I can't get enough of you, baby." His possessive words dug right into my chest, but I knew it was just the heightened state of passion that had made him say them. As much as I'd told him I didn't want to be owned, existing for Colt and Colt alone didn't seem all that bad. It was stupid and I hated myself for thinking it, but it sounded perfectly reasonable while he was inside of me.

"Colt, hold me. Don't let me go. Don't ever let me go."

His grip tightened, and I moved faster, pulling his cock into my pussy with each pass of my hips. My thighs trembled with fatigue from being fucked all night. It was a delicious pain that was only rivaled by the ache in my pussy from having him inside of me so often, thrusting into me with a fury that I'd never felt before. A fury that made me believe that he truly wanted to possess me. He needn't have tried so hard. At the moment, I wanted nothing more than to submit to every one of his commands. My pussy tightened and my thighs squeezed against him.

"That's it, beautiful. Come for me. Show me how much you want this."

I held his arms as shuddering waves of pleasure wracked my body.

"Fuck yeah, baby." He pushed into me making the orgasm last even longer. My head swayed back, and I held onto his arms for support as he pushed his cock into me. My pussy milking him with each thrust until his hot seed filled me.

I dropped down over him, whimpering with exhaustion, a fatigue that made my whole body ache contentedly. I rolled down next to him, and he cradled me in his arms, arms that made me feel both safe and wanted for the first time in my entire life.

He kissed me on the forehead. "Holy shit," he sighed. "I hope you realize what you've gotten yourself into. I can't get enough of you."

"Promises, promises," I teased. Deep down, I was thinking, wouldn't it be wonderful if it were true.

FIFTEEN
COLT

The wave coasted beneath us, and my feet temporarily left the sandy bottom. The water was cold, too cold to be out body surfing without a wetsuit, but I'd needed something to cool me down. Still, even while I was trying to cool myself down, I was watching the girl who had set my blood on fire.

Jade and Amy were sitting on their towels sipping sodas and laughing wildly about something. Slade had heard that some decent wave sets were expected and he'd talked me into bodysurfing. Prying me out of bed had taken some effort. I'd wanted to stay there all day with my naked and willing new friend. Friend. Hell, that term sounded more fucking crazy every time it went through my head. Jade had found a way to reach into my soul. I couldn't stop thinking about her, watching her, wanting her. I'd definitely never had a friend like that.

"Damn, bro, you haven't taken your eyes off her for a second," Slade's voice cut through my thoughts. "Never seen you like this. After that fucking marathon last night, almost thought you'd be bored by now."

"Nope."

"She's really gotten to you, huh?"

"Yep."

"Jeez, I think you went at it a little too hard last night. Can't get more than one syllable words out of you." Slade took off on a wave and shot in toward the shore. I followed on the next crest.

The section of beach wasn't visible from the highway, and there was no public parking. It was also a steep hike through some grassy weeds to get to the sand. Except for a few hardcore surfers and a couple walking their dog, the place was deserted.

Jade looked up and smiled as Slade and I walked toward them.

Amy held up her phone. "Just in time. Hunter's looking for you guys. Who wants to talk to him?"

Slade ignored her and flopped belly down on his towel. I dried my hand and took the phone.

"The reception is shitty out here," Amy said.

I sat in front of Jade. She ran her fingers over my scars. Normally, it bothered the hell out of me if a girl touched them or mentioned them, but it wasn't that way with Jade. The scars were a part of me, and I wanted her to know everything about me, even my ugly, shitty past. I knew she understood. She immediately wrapped her sun-warmed body around me.

"Ah, soft, hot titties pressed against my cold skin. That's better than any blanket."

She kissed my shoulder. That small gesture sent my pulse racing. Immediately, my cock tightened.

I put the phone against my ear. "What?"

"Been trying to reach you," Hunter said. He'd ridden up the coast with some other biker friends. They liked playing pool at some dive off the highway. I could hear loud voices and the clatter of cue balls in the background.

"Well, you reached me."

"I'm out here at Fink's Pool Hall and got to talking to a few of the guys who are regulars. They said some mean looking assholes were hanging around at Fink's yesterday asking about a missing girl. They were spouting off about some ten thousand dollar reward for finding her. They showed me the picture the men left them. It was Jade." I turned around and kissed her before standing up. I walked down toward the water. The reception grew worse, but I didn't want Jade to hear.

"Did they recognize the guys at all? Was one of them the bookie?"

"Didn't sound like him. No one had ever seen the guys before. You think he hired some private eye or something? The dick had money. That's for damn sure."

"Don't know, but now I'm worried about Jade working over at Lazy Daze. They might be scouring all the coastal hangouts looking for her, and ten thousand would sound pretty nice to a lot of people."

"She's not exactly the kind of girl who can fade into the crowd either."

I looked up the beach toward Jade. Her light hair shimmered in the sunlight, and her white smile sparkled as she laughed at something Slade said. "Nope, she definitely doesn't fade."

"You going to tell her?" Hunter asked.

"Not sure."

"And some more bad news. We've got to make another drop tomorrow. I told Rincon about the motherfucker they've got on the other end now, but he just laughed. Said if we wanted to give up the gig, he had plenty of people waiting to step in. Like I said, a little more time and we can start investing in more legit prospects."

"You mean like the kind where your business acquaintances don't shove their fucking Glocks into your skull?"

"A little longer, Colt. Just a little longer. Hey, we're going to hang out here for a few more games. Are you going to Stokey's party tonight? Or maybe you won't be able to take your dick out of Jade long enough to step out."

"What the fuck do you want from me, Hunter?"

"Nothing. Not a damn thing. Just seems like you're getting wrapped up tight in this thing, and she obviously comes with a lot of baggage."

"You just worry about your own fucked-up life, and I'll worry about mine."

"Yeah, yeah. Sore subject. I get it. Talk to you later."

I walked back up toward the towels. I'd bought Jade a bathing suit on the way to the beach. It was pale blue and hugged her curves just right, and all I could think about was taking it off of her.

I handed Amy the phone.

Slade looked up over his shoulder. "What did he want?"

I shook my head, letting him know that it wasn't anything I wanted to bring up in front of Amy and Jade. When the time was right, I'd let Jade know about the reward. But for now, I had no intention of letting her out of my sight. She had the night off tonight, but I would tell her before her next shift. If everything went smoothly on our drop tomorrow, I'd be back in time to head over to Lazy Daze for some beers. Lucky for me, she was working at my usual hangout.

I lowered my hand for her to take. "There are some cool tide pools on the other side of that outcropping of rocks. Feel like taking a walk?"

She slipped on the sandals she'd picked to go with the bathing suit. I liked the idea that I'd bought her everything she was wearing. It was stupid and cocky and I couldn't even explain it, but I liked it. She'd warned me that the one thing she didn't want was to be owned, and yet, all I could think about was that I wanted her to be mine and mine alone. No woman had ever gotten into my head that way, and I didn't mind. I was in no mood to fight it.

Hand in hand, we walked to the rocks that jutted out from the cliffs and into the sea. It was a place where sea lions, pelicans and giant crabs came to soak up the sun and pick up tasty morsels carried in by the tide. I climbed onto the first rock and turned around to help her up.

"They're slippery, and there are a lot of deep cracks, so watch where you step."

She stared down at the small pools created by the natural indentations in the rocks. When the tide came in, little fish and crabs filled the puddles. Jade crouched down. "These little guys have their own little ocean right here on this rock." She watched the tiny fish scooting around in their mini habitat.

I reached in and scooped up a tiny crab. She reached over and touched it. "It's amazing to think all these little worlds exist right in the midst of our own world."

"When we were younger, Slade and I used to spend hours out here trying to catch critters. Our shoulders would have big red blisters from the sun. We'd never catch much, but we never got discouraged."

I straightened. Again, I offered her my hand. Her hand felt small and frail in my grasp as I led her across the rocks. We jumped off onto the soft wet sand, and I led her to a massive crevice in the cliffs. We stepped inside.

Jade looked up and spun around, looking like an excited little girl. We were nearly completely surrounded by towering walls created by bands of shale and sandstone. The air inside the roomy fissure was cold. Jade wrapped her arms around me to get warm.

"Seems like I'm always stealing your body heat," she said. "This place is cool. It's so—"

"Private? Remote? Hidden from everyone's prying eyes?"

She smiled up at me. "Colt Stone, what do you have in that dirty mind of yours?"

I slid my hand into her bikini bottoms. "I think you know. It's been a helluva long time since you've been naked in my arms, and frankly, I'm dying to get between your thighs again." I pushed the suit, and it dropped to her ankles.

"It's been three hours at the most. Shit, you're right. That is a long time. But we're out in the open." She reached down to grab the bikini bottoms, but I caught her wrist.

"We're standing in a mountain, and no one's around. Most people don't even know about this place."

She raised a brow at me. "And just how do you know about it, or should I ask?"

I lifted her chin. "You shouldn't ask." I lowered my mouth to hers. Her lips parted instantly. She was always so willing, so ready, that it made me want her that much more. I reached down between her legs. She mewled against my mouth as my fingers slid through the folds of her pussy. It was slick with moisture. "Hmm, baby, is that for me?"

"Uh huh," she said softly. "It's all for you, Colt."

"Step out of those bikini bottoms, baby. I have to have you right this fucking minute."

She stepped free of her bikini. I pulled her hands out to the sides and stared down at her. She looked so tiny and vulnerable within the steep, massive walls of the crevice.

I dragged my gaze away from her sweet pussy. She

looked a little uneasy, but her blue eyes were dark with need. And I knew that need was throbbing between her legs. "Ask me, baby. Tell me what you want. I want to hear it from those perfect, plump lips."

"I want you, Colt," she said so softly it was nearly lost in the rock cavern.

"What do you want, darlin'? Tell me."

"I want you to fuck me." She wrapped her arms around my head and kissed my neck and chest. "Shit, I want you so badly, Colt, it's all I can think about. You inside of me, holding me, kissing me," her voice wavered. "I can die today if I can die naked in your arms." A quiet sob bubbled from her mouth. I took hold of her face and gazed down at her. Her blue eyes were wet with tears.

"Shh, baby, no tears." I held her against me. "It's what I want too. It's like you've reached inside my chest and taken hold of my heart. If you ever let go, I'm going to fucking die."

I kissed her long and hard. Her body trembled in my arms, but it wasn't from the cold.

I took her hand and turned her toward the hard rock wall. I pressed both of her hands up against it. "Spread your legs for me, baby. I have to be inside of you. I can't wait one second longer." I untied my swim trunks and pushed them down. My cock jutted toward her, begging to be sheathed in her tight pussy. A small gasp of excitement shot from her mouth as I reached down and pulled her ass out farther. Her hands scooted lower on the rock wall. "Hold on, baby." I grabbed her hips. Her cry echoed off the walls as I plunged inside of her.

"Fuck yeah, that's it," I growled. "This is where I need to be. Right here inside of you." I reached around and pressed my hand against her pussy. She squealed with pleasure as my thumb massaged her clit.

Her moans of pleasure echoed off the walls and filled my head bringing me closer to climax. "God, the sounds you make are so fucking hot, baby. I swear I'm going to make a recording on my phone so I can listen to you all the time." I rocked against her as she braced her hands on the rock and pushed her ass out farther. One hand massaged her clit while I brought the other one around to her ass. It was smooth and round under my palm. I slid a finger toward the tight, puckered hole. She gasped as I shoved my finger into her ass. In seconds, she was pushing harder against the pressure to take in more of it. I had all of her in my hands.

My assault came hard and fast as I jammed into her. Her thin arms looked as if they might snap. "Should I ease off, baby?" I doubted that I could, even if she said yes.

"No. I want more," she begged. She was fucking wild and completely willing and that made me crazy to have more of her. My finger plunged deeper into her ass.

She clenched my other hand between her legs as she ground her clit against my thumb.

Yes!" she screamed. Her pussy tensed around my hand, and her body shuddered almost uncontrollably as she came. Her fingers were white as she gripped for something to hold onto, something to keep her from sinking to her knees.

Her thin arms shook and I knew I needed to finish. I pulled my hand from between her legs and ass. My fingers dug into her hips as I pulled her against me so hard, sweet groans popped from her mouth. It was all I needed to hear. Her pussy gripped me tightly as my cock exploded in waves.

The second I pulled out, she fell back into my arms with a sigh. She didn't say a word as I wrapped my arms around her, pulling her back against my chest. We stood there in between the rock walls listening to the thunder of the ocean outside and the beating of our hearts. We'd both gone into this as an escape from reality, a good time without the brittle heartstrings between us. But, in reality, we both knew this was going way past a good time. Her tears just a few minutes before had assured me she was feeling the same way as me, as if there was more than just strings between us. We were feeling this with every fucking fiber of our being.

SIXTEEN

JADE

I wasn't completely thrilled about going to a party with Colt. If Amy hadn't been going, I would have probably stayed home. It would be all the people he knew, and I'd be sharing him with others. I wasn't completely convinced he was ready to share me with people either.

I sensed this more the second we walked into the packed house. I knew from the reactions of people whenever I went somewhere with Colt that he garnered a hell of a lot of attention from others. Some good, some bad, some just plain fearful. But he took it in stride, and I was beginning to as well. Only now, it seemed the entire noisy crowd had stopped their conversations and activities as we stepped inside the house. Hunter and Slade walked in too and, just like Colt, they seemed to expect that people would watch them. It seemed as if even the volume on the speakers pounding out music from every corner of the room had dimmed their sound as the three brothers strolled through.

Amy sensed my discomfort and grabbed my hand. "The girlie drinks are usually in the kitchen." It felt as if every head turned as she pulled me through the maze of party guests. In our fleeting excursion through the house, I glimpsed the girls who had come into Lazy Daze the night that Colt had grabbed the guy for touching me.

There were several people in the kitchen, a guy and three girls pouring bright red drinks from a blender. The guy had a black fedora pulled low on his head and a sleeve of tattoos on his right arm. "Aimster, you made it," he said. "I guess that means the Stone brothers aren't far behind."

"I'm sure they're already out back filling their cups with beer," she said.

The guy lifted his face and smiled at me from beneath the brim of his fedora. "And who is this little doll?"

"This is Jade. She's staying with Colt for awhile, but we're going to be roomies eventually." Amy smiled at me.

"Staying with Colt? Interesting." He handed me a drink. "Welcome to my home. I'm Stokey."

One of the girls standing in the kitchen overheard our conversation and turned around. She looked at me. "Are you Colt's girlfriend?" she asked. The simple question prompted giggles from her two friends. "Damn, just saying the name Colt and the word girlfriend in the same sentence sounds weird." She looked me over once with a bit of a sneer and then laughed again. "I guess you're just one in a long line, so have fun while it lasts."

"All right, you girls take your drinks and your bitchy remarks out of the kitchen." Stokey shooed them out. "Sorry about that. Guess Colt has left too many bitter women in his wake. Enjoy the party." He walked out, leaving Amy and me alone in the kitchen to sip our overly sweet drinks.

"Ignore that. Hannah has always had a big thing for Colt. I swear she used to follow him around in high school just trying to get him to notice her."

"I'm not bothered by it." I took a sip. Amy laughed at the puckered face I made. "Not the best drink I've ever had, but it beats beer out of a keg." I leaned against the counter. "Is it just me, or does everyone in this town gawk and stare whenever a Stone brother makes an appearance?"

Amy walked over to the table and grabbed a bottle of rum. "It'll cut down on that gross fruit punch taste." She poured some in her drink and then offered me the bottle. "You're not imagining it. Those boys are sort of notorious in this town. People are afraid of them, and at the same time they respect them. Everyone knows they grew up with a monstrous father, a man that everyone hated, but I think at the same time, everyone feels a little guilty about ignoring it. They were so damn afraid of Hank Stone, the dad, that no one dared speak up to him about the way he was raising his kids. Although, raising them was hardly the phrase for it. It's a fucking miracle they all lived to adulthood."

"So the fear of the dad rubbed off on the sons?"

"A little, but mostly people just know you don't cross them. That childhood made them tough. You don't get into a fight with any one of the Stone brothers unless you want to end up hurting real bad." Amy talked about them with a glint of pride in her eyes. I knew she loved them, and it was obvious they would do anything for her. Her relationship with Hunter was confusing and a little strange, but something told me, if he caved just slightly, they'd be together. Like their surname, the brothers had rock hard exteriors, and it seemed nothing short of a stick of dynamite could blow through their solid outer shells.

Just like Amy and Hunter had a complicated relationship, I'd formed a complex and somewhat disconcerting connection with Colt. As much as I tried to tamp down any emotional involvement with him, I could feel the threads of my heart beginning to fray. It wouldn't take much tugging from Colt to unravel me completely. I'd walked into his room with the unusual proposition, confident that I could handle a casual, no strings relationship. But the more I was with him, the more I doubted my own strength.

"They've got the bonfire going." Amy picked up her drink and stirred it with her finger. She licked it and added another shot of rum to her cup. "Let's go see what all the annoying people are up to, and by annoying, I mean the Stone brothers. As irritating as they are, I'd rather be talking to them than anyone else in this whole damn town."

We stepped out onto a brick patio that had a strand of chili pepper shaped lights strung from one post to the next. A small retaining wall of cinderblocks had been crudely built into a sitting wall. A blazing copper fire pit sat in the center.

I glanced around. Even with the poor lighting and thin veil of smoke hovering over the entire yard, it was easy to spot Colt and Hunter. Their shoulder spans were twice that of any of the other guys standing around with plastic cups of beer. They were also a good head taller than most. Hunter, in particular, made everyone else look miniature. Several of the girls who had joined them at Lazy Daze were talking to the brothers. The girl who had quickly climbed into Colt's lap that night was now clinging to his side stealing sips of his beer. But even as she drank from his cup, his intense green gaze followed me across the yard.

"Damn," Amy said with a chuckle, "that boy doesn't take his eyes off of you."

I held back a smile. Even though I'd warned him I didn't want to be owned by another man, I reveled in the idea that Colt was always watching me.

"I've never seen him act like this, Jade. What the heck did you do to him?"

"Nothing. We just reached a fun little agreement."

"Fun? Right. Slade said you two have been going at it like fucking rabbits."

I blushed and took a sip of my drink to avoid having to respond. She pointed to a spot on the wall near the fire. I sat down next to a nice looking guy, the kind of guy you'd want to bring home to impress your parents, if you had some to impress.

The guy smiled at me, and I thought he could be in a toothpaste ad with his perfect smile. He leaned forward. "Hey, Amy, are you going to introduce me to your new friend?"

Amy shrugged. "Jade, this is Zach." It seemed that Zach wasn't high on Amy's list of likable people.

"Nice to meet you, Jade. Are you visiting?"

"Actually, I'm staying for awhile. I'm working over at Lazy Daze."

His mouth tightened with disapproval. "That dive? You're too good for a place like that."

Amy leaned forward. "God, Zach, still the pompous douchebag you've always been."

"Coming from you, I consider that a compliment." Zach turned back to me. "When did you arrive in town? And why haven't I seen you?"

Before I could answer, he reached up and took a strand of my hair between his fingers. "You're hair is like spun gold."

Amy snickered at his comment. Then she elbowed me. "This should be good."

I followed the direction of her gaze. Colt was already across the yard, coming through the wall of chalky smoke before I'd barely turned my head. He stood like a menacing giant glowering down at Zach, who shrank back instantly.

"Hey, Colt," he said with a hoarse voice. "What's going on? Oh shit, are you with her? Didn't know," he said quickly as if he was begging for his life. "My mistake." Zach got up and walked quickly away.

Colt glanced at his retreating back. "Damn, was it something I said?"

"You don't need to say anything with that intimidating scowl, you big bully," Amy said. She hopped up as Colt sat down. "Speaking of big bullies, I think I'll go bug Hunter. Haven't seen him much today, and frankly, I'm behind on being irritating."

Colt pointed down to my drink. "Is it any good?"

"If you like rum-laced fruit punch, it's delicious." I lifted it for him to try, but he declined.

"Never mind. I'll let you drink it." He reached behind me and shoved his hand up the back of my shirt. "That way you'll be good and loose and drunk by the time we leave here."

"Yes, as opposed to the usual frigid, legs tightly crossed attitude I've been throwing your way. If I was any *looser*, you'd be scooping me off the floor with a damn spoon."

He smiled. "You're such a character. How can you be this gorgeous, this completely fuckable and still be such a character? Guess that's why you have me doing shit like lumbering across the yard to scare guys away from you."

"Yeah, about that."

"About what?"

"You huffing and puffing every time someone talks to me."

"You better get used to it, darlin'. I don't see me easing up on the huffing and puffing anytime soon."

"So, I'm not supposed to even talk to other guys?"

He gazed at me. I would have been more aggravated by his possessiveness if he wasn't so damn beautiful.

Everything about him made me want to submit to every unreasonable demand. Even though it was against everything I wanted and needed.

The rum was getting to my head, and I was in a teasing mood. Or maybe I just wanted to see how serious he was. "If I go over right now to that rather nice looking guy who is filling beer cups and flirt with him, what would you do? In front of all your friends and girls, most of whom you've no doubt slept with, what would you do?"

He stared down at me. His long dark lashes shaded the green in his eyes. "You testing me, darlin'? Don't bother. Look around. Do you see any guys talking to Street other than Hunter and Slade?"

I looked across the yard. The red chili lights were spinning in the breeze swirling through the yard. The same breeze had lifted away some of the bitter smoke spiraling up from the fire pit. Amy was standing next to Hunter. He was basically ignoring her as he bullshitted with everyone around him. No one was approaching Amy. With her copper hair and easy smile, she was easily the prettiest girl in the yard.

"Watch this. Hey, Mick," Colt called to a guy who was sitting on the opposite side of the fire. Colt reached into his pocket and pulled out his wallet.

Mick walked over. "Did you call me, Colt?" The guy looked completely surprised and slightly terrified.

"Yeah, I did." Colt plucked a twenty dollar bill from his wallet. He offered it to Mick. The guy stared down at the bill with plenty of confusion and a bit of trepidation.

"Thanks?" he said, and it was definitely a question.

Colt nodded. "That's yours. Now walk over and put your arm around Amy. It only has to be for a few seconds."

Mick looked across the yard toward Amy. Even in the glow of the fire, I could see his face blanch white. He smiled tentatively and handed the money back to Colt. "That's a good one, Stone." A nervous laugh followed. "You almost had me for a second." He walked away.

I looked at Colt. "Your brother basically ignores her and uses her for sex, but she can't talk to any other guy?"

"She could if there were any guys out there with balls big enough to talk to her."

Amy waved to me from across the yard. The ridiculous thing about it was she seemed perfectly happy just standing near Hunter.

I turned to Colt. "Your brother is an asshole, and I'm not your personal toy." I walked over toward the beer keg. I tossed the disgusting rum drink into the trash can and stepped up to the guy filling cups. He had a great head of hair and a sexy cleft in his chin.

I stuck my hands in my back pockets to accentuate my breasts and smiled. "Hey, can I get a cup?"

He glanced around anxiously. "Uh yeah, of course." He shoved the cup my direction, managing to slosh out half the contents in his haste.

I took the cup and stuck out my free hand. "I'm Jade."

"Hey, I'm Tucker."

"Tucker. That's a nice name." I was putting on my most charming expression and presenting my cleavage in the best possible light, but the guy was unmoved.

His eyes widened and a tall shadow splashed across the brick pavers beneath my feet. "Hey, Colt," he said nervously. "I was just giving her a beer."

I spun around. Colt stared down at me.

"Seriously?" I asked. "What? Were you sending death rays out of your eyes from all the way across the yard?"

Without warning, Colt lifted me and tossed me over his shoulder. "We need to have a little discussion out in the truck."

I smacked his back. "Hey, put me down, you big meanie." My head was spinning from the rum and from hanging upside down. "I might throw up all over your shirt."

Everyone turned and watched as Colt carried me out the front door and across the front lawn. I pounded his back. "I don't want to have a discussion."

I heard the truck door open. He plopped me into the

front seat. I shot back at him with my fists. "How dare you, you big jerk." I pounded him on the shoulders. He quickly had my wrists pinned together in one hand. "You're an asshole. You and your brother are just a couple of big fucking buttheads." My words were stretched by the alcohol. I struggled to free my hands, but his grasp was too strong. "I hate this. I hate that men are so much stronger and they can hurt you."

He released my wrists immediately. I peered up at him. His serious, hard expression had softened some. "That's not me, Jade. I'm not that guy. What he did to you—" the words stuck in his throat. "That's not me. I might be a jealous, overprotective jerk, but I would never hurt you."

I blinked back tears thinking about those words. "Hurt can come in a lot of different ways." I held his hand up to my beating heart. "Feel that. I can already feel it falling apart. Maybe this whole thing was a really bad idea."

He stared at me for a long moment, and I wasn't sure what to expect. "Yeah, a fucking bad idea," he muttered as he took hold of my face and covered my mouth with his. His kiss started out gentle and controlled, but as his tongue stroked my lips, coaxing them apart, the kiss grew more urgent. He took hold of me and lifted me over his lap. Sitting on my knees, I straddled him and wrapped my arms around his head to bring him closer. His hands slid down into my shorts, and once again, I melted into the trance, that space in time where the only thing that existed in the whole damn world was the man between my legs and my own body thrumming with need. I was still wearing shorts, but I ground my pussy against the fly of his jeans and the erection behind it straining to break free.

He pulled his mouth from mine. "What the fuck are we doing?"

I blinked down at him, feeling almost in despair at the notion that he didn't want to continue.

"The house is empty, and we're sitting in the front seat of the truck."

I smiled and slid off. I reached for my seatbelt. "Something tells me I should buckle up."

"Good thinking." He started the truck, and we tore off down the street as if someone had equipped the thing with jet thrusters.

The tires chirped as Colt turned into the driveway. We both nearly stumbled from the truck. Colt pushed open the front door, and before my feet could even take two steps inside, he had me in his arms.

His hungry kiss paused only to lift the shirt from my head. He threw it on the floor. He fumbled with the clasp on my bra and grunted in frustration. "Take that fucking thing off now." We were moving like two people who'd been denied sex for years rather than two people who'd already fucked four times that day. But the extreme want was there again. It never seemed to lessen. In fact, it seemed after every round of hot passion, I only wanted him more.

I reached back and unhooked the bra. He slid it off my shoulders and flung it across the room. He reached behind his neck and pulled his shirt up and over his head.

I took a deep breath. I'd seen him naked plenty of times, but every time he took off his shirt, I was awestruck. The power pulsing behind the black ink made me shiver with something I couldn't even explain. It was fear but a good fear. His extreme strength only served to excite me more.

"Strip naked, baby," he ordered. "I don't have the fucking patience to deal with buttons or zippers."

I took off my shorts. Then, teasingly, I turned around and pushed my panties to the ground. He groaned as I wiggled my naked ass at him. "See anything you like?" I asked.

"As a matter of fucking fact—"

I laughed wildly as his arms went around me, and he lifted me off my feet. "I'm going to fuck you in every corner of this house." He took me to the couch and dropped me onto my knees. I pressed my hands on the arm of the couch. He climbed on behind me. I expected him to fuck me with his cock but instead his mouth pressed against my pussy. He wasted no time coaxing juices from me. He lapped me up with a thirst that made me groan with need. His tongue pushed inside of me while his hand reached around and stroked my clit. His face was buried against me as I rocked back and forth on my knees to absorb all of it.

"I'm close, Colt, but I want your cock. I need all of it." Reluctantly, he pulled his mouth away. I felt the couch cushions move as he readjusted himself. A small cry of excitement squeaked from my lips as I waited anxiously for him to fuck me. Instead, he pressed just the hot wet tip of his cock against my pussy. Another sound, this one more desperate, left my mouth.

"Darlin' this is where you're supposed to beg. Tell me what you want."

"Fuck me, please, Colt. I want it. I want you. Fuck me now before I go mad from wanting you."

I cried out in relief and nearly lost my grip on the couch arm as he jammed his cock deep inside of me. It took no more than three deep thrusts, and my pussy clamped shut around him. "God yes, Colt!" My cries bounced off the walls.

My arms weakened beneath me. Suddenly, Colt's strong hands went around me. He pulled out, lifted me into his arms and carried me to the bathroom. "Told you, baby. I want to do it everywhere. Then I can think of you in every damn room. Not that I ever stop thinking about you anyway."

I stretched up and pressed my lips against his neck. "Damn good thing." He swung my legs around, and I used my foot to push open the bathroom door. As with every part of the house, the tile sink was cluttered with stuff. Still holding me in one arm, Colt swept his hand across the counter sending combs and deodorant and toothpaste into the sink.

He set me down on the counter. I sucked in a breath as my naked bottom touched the cold tile. He looked especially massive in the small bathroom. I watched with excitement as he pressed himself between my legs. His hands went around my ass as he lifted me and scooted me to the edge of the counter. He wrapped his hands under my knees and lifted them up to give him better access. I leaned back on my hands. He stared down at his cock as it plunged inside of me. He withdrew and impaled me again, watching hungrily each time as my pussy swallowed his long erection.

"Fuck, this is it, baby. I'm staying here just like this all night, watching you take me into that sweet, hot pussy." His eyes were dark green as he peered up at me through a dark curtain of lashes. "Goddamnit, Jade, what have you done to me? I'm gritting my fucking teeth, tense with the idea that I'll never have enough of you. I'm standing here buried deep inside of you, and I'm still worried it won't be enough."

His desperate words made my chest ache. I wrapped my legs around his waist and scooted closer to him. His powerful hands wrapped behind my ass, and he held me tightly against him as he ground into me as deep and far as he could get.

He leaned forward and kissed my mouth, groaning against my lips as he continued to slam against me. "If you ever deny me, darlin', I will break in fucking two."

"Never," I whispered. "I can never say no to you."

Again he pulled out of me. I nearly fell forward from disappointment. He carried me out of the bathroom.

I laughed. "Where to now?"

"Fuck the corners of the house, I want you in my bed."

I rested my head on his shoulder. "Thank goodness, that tile was really cold."

He laughed as he dropped me onto the center of his bed. He grabbed some of the lotion we'd been using. We'd been going at it so long and so hard, I was getting tender.

Colt's gaze coasted over my naked body as he filled his palm with the liquid. He rose up on his knees, and I caressed his stiff, swollen erection as he pressed the creamy liquid between my legs. It immediately felt cool and soothing. The ache he'd created had been worth every minute.

My eyes drifted shut as he massaged the lotion in between the folds of my pussy. "Do you like that, baby?"

"Yes," I said on a long, whispery sigh.

Then his liquid coated fingers slid down underneath me. His fingers trailed along the crack of my ass and into the tight hole. I shifted my hips up to accommodate his finger. He impaled my ass as his mouth cover my breast. With his tongue, he drew teasing circles around my taut nipple as he pushed his finger into my anus.

"Touch yourself, baby." His words sounded deep and gritty.

I looked up at him.

"You can never say no, baby, right? Prove it to me. I want you to show me that you'll do anything I ask."

I moved slowly at first, slightly embarrassed about the idea of touching myself in front of him. My hand reached down to my pussy. He gazed down at me as I touched myself. Having him watch me was far more erotic than I could have imagined. In a few minutes, I was lost in the delirium of physical arousal as he shoved his finger in my ass and I massaged my clit.

Without removing his finger he gently turned me onto my side. As I pulled my hand from between my legs, he placed it back on my pussy. He scooted down behind me and kissed my neck and my shoulders. His breath grew more ragged, and I could tell something had changed.

He leaned down to my ear. "I want all of you, Jade." I sucked in a breath as he removed his finger and pressed the tip of his cock against me. "Anything, darlin'?" He pushed the tip in. I clenched at first, but then he trailed more luxurious kisses along my neck making me relax. "It's only because I want you so bad, baby." He pushed in farther. "Keep touching yourself. Make yourself come, darlin'. I want to hear that cry of ecstasy coming from those perfect lips."

I did as he asked and soon found myself moving against his cock as he pushed deeper inside of me. My mind was in a haze. It felt as if every cell in my body was being stimulated. I tightened my legs around my hand, and he slid in deeper, as if he would pierce right through me. It was a delicious pain that I might not have enjoyed if it hadn't been Colt. My heart was behind my words. I would never deny him anything. I just wanted him with me, connected in any way possible. Even this. I brought myself to the edge and as he pushed deeper, I came in trembling waves. I cried out as he finished by pushing himself inside of me. His fingers gripped my hips and he held me against him. A deep, long groan of satisfaction rolled up from his chest.

We melted together in a hot heap as our breathing returned to normal. Every part of me ached with sweet delight. The feeling only intensified as he wrapped his big arms around me and held me tightly against his chest. He kissed the back of my shoulder.

"My beautiful, willing Jade," he said quietly. "I know you said you don't want to be owned by any man, but just let someone try and take you from me. No fucking way I'm ever letting you go."

With those words and within his protective embrace, I fell fast asleep.

SEVENTEEN

COLT

After the last drop when the jerk on the other end had pushed his gun against my head, I was less than anxious to meet up with their boat. Dark clouds colored the horizon a chalky gray, and the looming storm churned up the sea enough to toss around our thirty foot trawler.

Their boat was an old yacht that had been converted into a much sleeker, faster version of its original self. We'd been delivering drugs to some wealthy creep who had connections to the gambling casinos down south. Even though we had no idea where the blow went after it left our hands, the quality and the price of the stuff seemed to indicate that it was going to rich people, people who spent their days trying to figure out how to get more thrills out of life. I, for one, didn't care where it ended up as long as we got paid and as long as things went off without a hitch. Something told me that was no longer possible with the new man in charge.

His black shades were the first thing we saw as he and his two sidekicks climbed up the rope ladder. He had his shoulder holster strapped down tight under his coat.

Hunter moved closer to me. We had our guns tucked under our shirts, ready and loaded, in case this guy had a problem with the cargo or if he just went nuts in general. That seemed highly likely with the way he was grinning at us like the Joker from Batman.

"This motherfucker sure rubs me the wrong way," Hunter muttered from the side of his mouth. This time Slade came down without being asked. Safety in numbers.

"Gentlemen," he said as if we were all meeting for a friendly chat, "it looks like Mother Nature is going to be heavy handed today." He swept his arm around at the ever darkening sky. "So, without further ado—" He yanked his gun out as if he was pulling out his wallet. He pointed it at me. "You know my policy. Until everything is counted and tested, I need a sacrificial lamb, and that's you, Hollywood."

My fists tightened but they would be no match for his gun. As badly as I wanted to pull mine, I didn't like the idea of dying in a bloody gun battle at sea all over a shipment of coke. Especially when now I had someone waiting for me, someone who needed me. Someone who I needed just as badly.

He walked over and pressed the gun to my head. Red hot rage flickered in my brothers' faces. I shot them a look of warning. This would be a bad fucking time for someone to lose their temper. And, if nothing else, Rincon was always consistent with the quality of the cargo.

We stayed at the stern while Hunter watched the water for other boats. Slade led the two men to the cargo hold to check the bundles for quantity and quality. My life was in Rincon's hands at this point. Something told me the asshole with his gun to my head wouldn't hesitate if his partners came up from the hold with bad news.

"Colt Stone," he said, and I peered sideways at him. "Don't look so shocked. It was easy to find out who owned this ugly fishing boat. I've been asking around about you. They call me Ace. Just to keep things balanced."

"Why the fuck would you be asking around about me? And who the hell are you asking?"

"Don't worry, I've been in this business long enough to know how to keep things discrete and smooth. You impress me as the kind of man who keeps his cool when shit is going down. I need someone like you. Those two clowns I'm traveling with are worthless. You can make a lot more money on the other side of this drop. I'll see that you get a better cut."

"Yeah, I don't think so. I'm good on this side."

A short, harsh laugh made the gun barrel bounce against my head. "See, that's what I like about you, Stone. A bullet is just a few inches from your brain, but you didn't even hesitate in telling me no. That's guts."

Hunter was keeping watch through his spyglass, but I knew his attention kept flicking our direction. This new addition to the job, where my life was on the line with every drop, seemed to be making him reconsider our line of work.

The gun moved against my temple as Ace reached into his pocket for something. He pulled out a piece of paper. "By the way, I was hanging out at a bar at the marina and saw this on the wall. The ten thousand caught my interest. The reward is just for information leading to the girl. Sounds like some easy money." He unfolded it. It was a flyer with Jade's picture offering a reward for finding her. I kept up a solid expression even though my heart was thumping hard against my ribs.

"What do you want from me?" I asked coolly.

"Just thought since you live near the marina, you might know the girl. You look like the type of guy who scores pretty well in the chick department."

"Nope, don't know her."

"Just thought I'd ask. Figured it would be a quick ten thousand bucks." He glanced down at Jade's picture with a sick grin, and I wanted to rip it from his hands. "Shit, I'd like to hit that, eh? Bet she has a fine little cunt to go with that pretty face."

My pulse was pounding in my head, and I briefly wondered how fast I could grab his gun and turn it on his ugly motherfucking face.

"I mean ten thousand bucks— she must be quite a fuck." His dry laugh startled me. He noticed my sudden tension. "Damn, maybe you're not as steady and confident as I thought, Stone." He looked at the picture and then at the side of my face. It had been impossible not to react to his comments. Now he sensed something was wrong.

After a long, tense minute, he returned the paper to his pocket. "Knew it was a long shot. But I did hear that you've been seen hanging around with a beautiful girl with white blonde hair. Thought maybe she was the girl on the flyer."

"Told you, I don't know her."

Slade and the men returned carrying some of the bundles. I was relieved to see them.

"Are we good to go?" Ace asked.

"Yes, everything's fine."

Ace moved his face closer to mine before lowering

his gun. "You will let me know if you change your mind about my offer."

"Don't hold your breath."

He laughed. It was a harsh, grating sound. He put the gun back in the holster. I swallowed to relieve the dryness in my throat. It wasn't the gun pointed at me that had caused it. It was the reality that Jade's picture was everywhere. It was only a matter of time until some greedy asshole like the one standing on our deck caught sight of her. I needed to get home and tell Jade what was happening.

EIGHTEEN

JADE

Amy parked the car and we climbed out. The rich smell of coffee drifted around the parking lot. There were only a few people in the shop sitting around tables cradling steaming cups in their hands. Several coffee drinkers glanced up as we stepped inside. Two women, in particular, did a double take as if they knew Amy and me.

"Damn," Amy whispered, "do I have dirt on my face or something?"

"So it's not just me being paranoid?"

We got in line. I finally had a few dollars of spending money from tips, and I'd told Amy I wanted to buy her a coffee and muffin to repay her for being such a true friend.

"Oh good, they've got those little crumb cakes," Amy said. "Love to dip those in my coffee."

"How many do you want? My treat, remember? As long as we stay inside my five dollar budget."

"One is plenty. In fact, we could share it." She pulled out her phone. "A voicemail from Jack. I'll bet he needs one of us to come in earlier."

"I need to get a phone for myself. Someday."

"Hey, I've got to take a whiz. Tell them I want extra whipped cream." Amy pressed a button on her phone and walked away with it against her ear.

The girl behind the counter looked at me with round eyes, and I wondered what the heck was wrong this morning that was making people look at me as if I had horns growing from my head. Amy came scurrying out from the short hallway that led to the restrooms. She was holding a paper in her hand and looking as if a monster was chasing her from the bathroom.

"What the heck, Amy? Was there a spider in the stall or something?"

She grabbed my arm and spun me toward the door. "Forget the coffee. We need to get out of here." She led me quickly to the door.

"O.K. now you're freaking me out," I said as we raced across the parking lot to her car.

"Yeah? Well be prepared to be properly freaked."

She shoved the paper into my hand. "Someone pinned this to the bathroom door. Get in the car."

I climbed in. My heart was pounding as I unfolded the paper. My picture was staring back at me with the words *Missing* typed in bold print across the top. There was a short description below, but I was in no state of mind to read it. The word *Reward* and $10,000 were printed in red at the bottom of the flyer. I recognized the phone number. It was Ray's cell phone.

"Shit. Shit. Shit."

"Yep. Yep. Yep." Amy backed the car out of the spot.

"And I thought people were seeing horns coming from my head. Turns out they were seeing dollar signs."

"Ten thousand of them to be exact," Amy said. She pulled the car out onto the road and headed back toward Colt's house. "That's from him, isn't it? The guy you're running from. Did you steal something from him?" she asked. I felt slightly hurt by the question, but it was a perfectly reasonable one considering the heft of the reward.

"Just his stupid ass pride. The last time we were together, he tried to strangle me. I think he's just pissed that I walked out on him."

"A wrecking ball to a big male ego. What an asshole."

I sank back against the seat and fought back the

tears that burned my eyes. "What am I going to do? I'm going to have to leave town."

"And go where? All alone? You're safer here with Colt. Then we can all look out for you."

"Amy, I don't want to put any of you in danger."

"Danger? Shit, the Stone brothers would eat dynamite for breakfast if they packed it in a cereal box." She shook her head. "No, you're definitely safer with us." She looked over and brushed a blonde hair off my face. "But I think we need to do some things to change your appearance."

I looked at her. "What do you mean?"

"That silvery white hair is too unusual." She closed an eye as if she was sizing me up for something. "With your blue eyes and suntanned skin, you'd make a beautiful brunette."

"Brunette?"

"Yep, brunette." She pulled into the parking lot of the drug store. "You'd better stay in the car while I buy the hair color." She reached into her backseat and fished around before sitting back up with a black cap. "Put this on, Goldilocks. I'll be right back." Her phone buzzed. "Wait, that's probably Jack. I forgot to listen to his voicemail. Hey, Jack, what's up?"

I could hear his baritone voice coming through her phone, but I couldn't make out the words. As he spoke, Amy looked at me. There was disappointment in her expression as she listened. She sighed dejectedly. "Yeah fine. All right. See you later." She hung up and stared down at the phone to avoid looking at me. But I already knew.

"He doesn't want me to work there anymore," I said.

"Someone pinned a flyer up in the hallway. He doesn't want any trouble. Big fucking coward. How the hell was he ever in the military?" She shoved her phone in my hand. "In case of emergency. The boys are number one, two and three. I'm sure you can guess which brother is number one, the big jerk."

"Here's the five I was going to use for the coffee." I placed the money in her hand, and she hopped out of the car. I watched as she hurried across the lot and disappeared into the store.

The first tear broke free. I stared down at the phone in my hand. How badly I wanted to talk to Colt, to sit in his protective arms and have him tell me that he would keep me safe. In the back of my head, I'd known that Ray wasn't going to just fade away and accept that he'd lost. But there was always that tiny sprig of hope that he would forget me and move on. This wasn't about wanting me back anymore. This was Ray refusing to admit defeat. He would rather part with a big chunk of money than admit that he'd lost me for good. My biggest worry was just how far the creep would go to get me back.

My finger swiped over the phone list. Colt was number three on speed dial. He and his brothers had gone out on their boat, and his mood had assured me it wasn't for a pleasure trip. All three brothers had looked rather grim as they trudged out the door this morning.

As I held the phone, it buzzed in my hand. I nearly dropped it. It was Colt. I hesitated thinking it was wrong for me to answer a call meant for Amy, but just seeing his name on the screen made the tears roll down my cheeks. I rubbed my thumb over it and lifted it to my ear. "Hello." My voice was small and quiet.

"Hey, Street, I need you to stay with Jade."

"It's not Stree— it's not Amy." I sobbed once and took a deep breath. "It's me."

"Jade? Are you with Amy?"

"Yeah, she went into the store. Colt, my picture is all over the place. Ray is offering a reward."

"I know."

I sobbed again.

"Don't cry, baby." Of course, having him say that and call me baby at the same time made me cry harder. "You're with me. I'm not going to let anything happen to you. You'll have to give up your job for now."

"That's not a problem." I sucked in a shuddering breath to get a grip on myself. "Someone put up the reward poster in Lazy Daze. Jack had to let me go."

"We're almost back at the dock now. Stay with Amy at our house. We'll have to figure out a plan."

I sniffled and nodded as if he might see me through the phone. The deep, confident sound of his voice had already lifted my spirits.

"No more tears. I'm going to take care of you, darlin'."

"Hurry back." I sniffled again. Amy came out of the store with the bag of hair dye.

She slid into the driver's seat, and I handed her the phone. "The guys are on their way back to the dock. Colt said not to worry."

"See, told you. I can tell you one thing, it's always a damn big bonus to have the Stone brothers on your side." She lifted a box from the bag. "Coffee brown? Figured since we didn't get to drink it, you could still wear it. We'll make you look so good, Colt won't be able to keep his hands off of you." She laughed. "Oh wait, that's already not a problem, is it?"

I reached over and hugged her. "God, Amy, I've never had a friend like you. Thank you."

She squeezed me back. "I'm glad you came here, Jade."

NINETEEN
COLT

Jade walked out of the bathroom with a towel wrapped around her head. She smiled and pulled the towel off. Her hair fell around her shoulders in dark brown strands. "What do you think?" she asked tentatively.

I pulled her into my arms just relieved to see her safe and in the house. "I think I have to start from the beginning with my new brunette girlfriend. And I'm looking fucking forward to it."

"Jeez, I don't know," Slade said. "She's pretty hard to look at anyhow, but as a brunette—" He crinkled his nose.

Jade balled up the towel and threw it at him.

Amy walked out of the bathroom with the empty

boxes of hair color. She stopped to admire her handiwork. "Looks pretty darn good if I do say so."

Jade smiled at her. "Amy was the brains behind the disguise. It was smart thinking."

"Where's Hunter?" Amy asked.

"The *Durango* was making a funny sound." Slade sat on the couch and lit a joint. Amy made a beeline for it. Slade held it up out of her reach. "Damn, Street, let me take a toke first, you little weed beggar."

I sat in the big, slightly ripped arm chair and pulled Jade down onto my lap. "I've been giving it some thought. I think we need to stay out at the cottage. A lot of people, people who have need for a lump of money, have seen you with me. Not many people know I own that old cottage, and it's out of the way. It's not visible from the highway or the town."

After Ace had shown me the picture, I'd started thinking about how I was going to keep her safe. She was an exceptionally pretty new face in a small town. I was sure the only thing that had kept anyone from calling the number on the flyer to claim the money was me. Most people in this town wouldn't dare cross me or my brothers. Not even for a nice chunk of cash. But that didn't mean that other people, strangers passing through or sketch-ass dicks like Ace, wouldn't be keeping a sharp eye out for her.

After Noddy died, her little house had sat there for

several years, stuck in a long family probate battle. When it finally came on the market, everyone else had forgotten about it. Everyone except me. I'd saved enough from our *business* to buy the thing outright. Now it would make the perfect hiding place.

"Are you sure about all this, Colt?" she asked. "I could just get on a bus and head across the country or something."

"Is that what you want?" Just asking the question made my heart sink in my chest. This had started as a no heartstrings proposal, but she'd already taken a firm hold of mine. I hadn't even known that I had any. She found them. Jade had managed to reach past the icy layers and find them.

"No, of course not, but I'm causing such an upheaval in your lives. If anything were to happen to any of you, I could never forgive myself."

Slade coughed once and squinted at us through a screen of smoke. "Some pansy-assed, loafer-wearing asshole who can throw cash around like it's fucking fairy dust is no threat to the Stone brothers. Danger is our middle name."

Amy laughed. "See? Told you they'd eat dynamite for breakfast if offered."

Slade raised his brow at her. "Now why the fuck would we eat dynamite?"

"It was just a colorful hyperbole— you know, an over-exaggeration to make a point," she said.

"A hyper bowly? What the fuck is that?" Slade grabbed the joint from her fingers. "Here, you've had too much of that. You're talking fucking nonsense."

Jade smiled and rested her head against my shoulder. "You're right. I couldn't possibly leave you guys. You're just too darn entertaining."

"Damn right. I'm going to load some things into the truck. You pack up what you'll need." I turned to my brother. "Slade, you guys need to go around town and yank down those flyers."

Slade nodded. "Hey, bro, I was thinking— maybe we should draw the snake out of his hole."

"You mean get him to show his face?" I asked.

He shrugged. "Might be able to put an end to this search fast if we give him a good scare." I could see the gears spinning in Slade's head. He thrived on this kind of shit.

"Maybe. But the man comes with his own army of pricks. We might start an all out war. We'll need to make a plan." I tightened my arm around Jade. "In the meantime, I need to hide my ten-thousand-dollar treasure."

TWENTY
JADE

There were still a few kitchen utensils and pieces of furniture that had been left behind in the cottage after Noddy's family had taken what they wanted. Colt had put his mattress and bedding into the truck along with an ice chest to keep food in. There was no refrigerator, but we'd make do. I'd spent some time sweeping the worn wooden floors, and Colt put in the two windows that had been next on his project list.

The bedroom still had an old nightstand and a pretty glass lamp with a frilly lampshade. Just from looking at Noddy's things and knowing how she had looked after the brothers in her own quiet way made me think I would have really liked her.

Colt came in with some driftwood and a smile. I could tell he was liking the idea of staying in his own place. "The electricity is on because I need it for my drills and tools, but the gas is off. So, no heat. But even without it, I think I can get a nice fire going in the hearth with this seasoned driftwood. Once the marine layer settles in at night, it gets pretty cold out here." He piled the wood next to the fireplace. Then he walked over and pulled me into his arms. "And, of course, there's always my infamous body heat that you're so good at stealing."

I wrapped my arms around him. "I do love your body heat and your body . . . for that matter. If I didn't have a madman hunting me down, staying holed up here with you would be close to the best thing that'd ever happened to me."

"Close to?" he asked.

"Well, the best thing that ever happened was me deciding to hide on your boat. A little decision that brought me straight into these arms."

He pressed his palm against the side of my face and kissed me. "I'd say my luck began when you decided to use me as your human shield in that hallway." He lowered his arms. "That reminds me." He walked out to the kitchen and returned with a bag. "I bought this stuff on the way home today."

I pulled out a phone.

"That's for your safety. I put all of our numbers in it, and Amy's, of course. Otherwise, I'd be hearing about it big time."

I turned it on. "Thank you. It actually makes me feel part of the human world again. Of course, I'm still trying to decide if that's a good or bad thing."

"I'm still on the fence about that myself. But lately, I've been landing on the side of good." He brushed a strand of brown hair off my face. It was strange seeing dark hair around my shoulders and face.

I reached in the bag. My fingers landed on silky fabric. I pulled it out. It was an extremely scant blue silk babydoll nightgown. "Hmm."

"Uh, yeah, that's got nothing to do with safety. That's for me," he said.

I held up the sheer confection of lace and silk and laughed. "You weren't embarrassed buying this thing?"

I peered up at him. His confident expression assured me he hadn't been.

"Right," I said. "I'm sure you've never been embarrassed in your life."

He dropped his gaze. "Not true. As a kid, on days like Halloween when everyone else was wearing their Superhero costumes and I had to go to school in the same ripped up jeans I'd been wearing all week, I was plenty embarrassed."

I curled my hand around his neck and kissed him. "I'm glad that time is over for you." I glanced toward the big picture window that had a great view of the ocean. Dusk was closing in fast. "The fog is rolling in. I think you should start the fire while I see how the gift fits."

"I'm looking very forward to seeing that myself."

I walked into the bedroom and changed. Without a mirror, it was hard to know how I looked, but the lingerie fit perfectly. I supposed after the marathon of sex, where we'd explored every inch of each other's bodies, he had a pretty good idea of my size. The silky fabric was nearly transparent. Thin, blue ribbons held the lightweight nightie on my shoulders. The two panels parted like lace curtains just below the bra line, and the matching panties were no more than a triangle of sheer blue lace held on by a thin waistband. Heat swirled through me as I thought about Colt looking at me in the sheer lingerie. Even though he'd seen me completely naked, somehow I felt even more exposed in the nearly transparent nightie.

Colt was leaning into the hearth poking at the lit kindling with a long stick. He'd carried in the mattress and blankets and placed them in front of the small, stone hearth. He had his laptop on the floor playing music, and there were some potato chips and beer next to it.

"Looks like a very sexy picnic," I said.

He turned around. His chest swelled with a long, deep breath.

I held out my arms and turned around once. "What do you think?"

"Damn." It was just the one word, but it was the way he'd said it that sent a tremor of excitement through me.

He stood up and made the room look exceptionally small. His size and the way he looked at me as he walked toward me made me extremely aware of just how vulnerable I was. "I'm defenseless when you're near, Colt. I can't think. I can't breathe. I can't even remember my life before I met you. I don't know if I've ever felt anything before this. I was just going through the motions of life to survive."

His big hands took hold of my arms, and he lifted me so that only my toes touched the floor. He dipped his head down and kissed me. "Seeing you stand here in the middle of this house looking like a fucking angel makes me want to pinch myself. If it turns out I'm sleeping and imagining this, then I'm going to be so fucking pissed."

"I'm real and this is real."

"It's so fucking real, baby, my head is spinning." He leaned down and kissed my breasts through the papery thin fabric of the lingerie. His hand reached beneath the two open panels, and his palm smoothed over my skin, making my knees weaken. I grasped his arms to stay upright.

"I want to melt into a puddle every time you touch me," I said between breaths.

He dropped down to his knees in front of me and

kissed my bare belly. His mouth trailed down to the small triangle of blue silk covering my pussy. He kissed me through the material. He ran his finger along the thin strand of fabric that ran up between my ass cheeks. A deep, shuddering sound thundered in his chest as his fingers reached the hot cream that already surged from my pussy.

"God, baby, I'm so hard it hurts. You're always so hot and ready and willing. Sometimes, I think I'm just going to fucking explode when you're near me."

He led me over to the mattress, and I stretched out on the blanket. The fire was just starting to crackle and pop with life as the salt dried wood glowed with heat. Its comforting warmth flowed over my scantily clad body, but it was nothing compared to the heat coming from Colt's body as he knelt down next to me.

He reached back and pulled off his shirt.

"When you pull off your shirt, I swear my heart takes a couple extra beats."

"Yeah?" He smiled. "I like that."

I reached for the button on his pants, but he took hold of my wrist. Then he grabbed my other wrist and with his big hand he pinned my arms against the pillow above my head. He traced the lacy trim of the babydoll with a callused fingertip. "You're so fucking beautiful. Every curve, every inch of your creamy skin, everything about you makes my cock hard." He held my hands securely as his free hand trailed down my stomach to the risqué panties. He watched my face as his fingers slid beneath the tissue thin fabric and into the slick folds of my pussy. The tattoos on his massive arm twitched and moved as he stroked me deep inside, as always, finding the spot that nearly took me right off the cliff of an orgasm. But he was skilled. When he sensed I was close, he backed off to keep me aroused.

I groaned and pushed my pussy against his hand wanting to take in more. "God, it's sweet fucking torture, Colt, how close you take me every time." I tried to free my hands. I wanted to touch him. I wanted to take his hard cock in my hand and press it down between my legs.

He smiled wickedly at my struggle but tightened his grip on my wrists. "Watching you squirm like this in that hot little nightie is making me fucking nuts."

He plunged another finger into me and lowered his mouth to mine. "Darlin', do you trust me?" His green eyes sparkled with mischief. I trembled as he spoke.

"Yes?" It came out as a question.

Colt laughed. He leaned forward and took my bottom lip between his teeth. He bit it lightly, and I tensed at first. I'd only ever felt safe in his arms. I knew he would never hurt me. So far, every time he'd touched me had been pure, unimaginable pleasure. Sensations so intense that he'd managed to get a firm hold on my heart. He'd become the center of my life so fast, I hadn't even had time to realize it until right this second.

"Yes, I trust you."

He released me and pulled his hand from between my legs. I sighed in disappointment. He stared down at me as he lifted the end of his bed sheet. He ripped off a strip of fabric. With one tug of his strong hands, another strip came off.

I got up on my elbows. "What the heck are you doing?"

A crooked grin deepened the creases running along the side of his mouth. He didn't respond as he tossed the strips of cloth over his shoulder. He stood up and walked over to the pile of Noddy's things that were stacked in the room. He reached in and pulled out a ladder back chair. It was dusty and a little warped. He placed it close enough to the fire to catch the warmth. His mouth twisted in thought as he seemed to be assessing the roping across the seat of the chair. He walked over and grabbed a pillow from the mattress.

After setting the pillow on the chair, he motioned me over to him. Tentatively, I got up and tiptoed across the mattress and onto the floor where he stood like the world's most beautifully carved man.

"Turn around," he said sharply. I hesitated, and he raised a brow at me. He pushed my chin up and kissed my mouth. "You won't deny me, darlin', will you? Anything, remember?"

The commanding words made me sway on my feet. He took hold of my arm and turned me around so that my back was to him. He reached up with a strip of cloth and wrapped it around my eyes. I sucked in a breath and touched the fabric. He took my hand and pulled it away. I'd told him I trusted him, and in my heart, I knew I did.

Relax, I told myself. The tension slowly drained from my body. I couldn't see anything but the slight flicker of light coming from the fireplace. This time, with a gentler touch, he turned me around and backed me up so that the chair was behind my legs. I sat down.

I heard his heavy footsteps and felt the heat trailing from his body as he walked behind the chair. He took hold of my hands and pulled them behind the back. The strip of fabric wrapped around them.

"Colt," I said, and was shocked by the worry in my tone.

He came around the front of the chair and knelt in between my thighs. His palms took hold of my face.

"Colt," I said again. I wasn't sure if I was trembling from fear or excitement. It seemed to be a mixture of both.

"Shh, darlin'. You're safe with me." I startled at first as his mouth covered my breast. He teased and licked and kissed my nipples through the silky fabric. At first, I pulled at the bindings wanting to be free to touch him, but then my captivity and my lack of sight started pushing me to another level of erotic emotion that I'd never felt before. I was his to do with as he pleased, and I wanted it. I wanted all of it.

His words were true. I felt safe with him, safe enough to drift into a glorious haze of sexual desire the likes of which I'd never experienced before. He was all power, menacing power, and he had complete control and I loved it. I loved him. I wasn't going to say no to him because I would do anything he asked.

He drew his hot mouth down the skin of my belly, then I heard him sit back. His strong hands pushed my thighs apart. He kissed my inner thigh in a long, sensual trail. My head dropped back against the chair. I was completely relaxed, lost in the feel of his mouth on my skin.

His warm breath blew against my pussy. My bottom fidgeted on the pillow as his fingers reached up and pushed aside the tiny piece of material separating his touch from the naked, wet folds. He spread me wide open and groaned as his mouth pressed hungrily against my pussy.

"Holy shit," I sighed as his tongue dove inside of me and swirled around in the moisture pooling between my legs. His fingers held me open as his tongue continued its erotic penetration. Unable to move from the chair, I leaned back and absorbed it all. I couldn't see him or touch him, but I felt his presence with the intensity of a thunderstorm, frightening and thrilling, all in one moment of complete ecstasy.

He lifted my legs and dropped them over his strong shoulders to gain even more access to my pussy. I was already totally exposed and completely at his mercy.

With deliberate, skilled patience, Colt brought me to orgasm. The tightening started in my pussy and traveled through my entire body. "Yes, Colt!" It felt as if I would splinter into a million pieces to be swept away by the ocean breeze. The pulsing waves seemed to last forever. I whimpered with exhaustion at the end of it all.

Colt placed my feet on the ground and slid my bottom so that my pussy hung off the edge of the chair. I had no idea what was happening, but my body quivered with anticipation. He pushed his long hard cock inside of me. I cried out again as my pussy clenched around him in one long orgasm. The chair rocked beneath me as he thrust deep inside of me.

"I know you don't want to be owned, baby," his voice was hoarse, and it seemed he was close to coming. "But you are mine. You are mine, Jade." A low grunt echoed through the room as he spilled his hot seed inside of me.

He collapsed down over my lap and reached around to my hands to untie them. I lifted my hand and pushed down the blindfold. He leaned over me with his head on my lap and his broad bare back beneath my hands. I smoothed my fingers over the thin, long ridges of scars that crisscrossed his skin. The sight of them produced a painful lump in my throat. He flinched at first but then relaxed under my touch. His head remained in my lap. His jeans had been pushed hastily down below his hips, and his rock hard ass was exposed. Just like the rest of the man, it was pure perfection.

"Do they hurt?" I asked as I caressed the scars.

He shook his head without lifting it from my lap. "Only in my soul."

I swallowed to relieve the tightness in my throat and chest.

Colt lay there hunched over me, completely silent and unmoving as I smoothed my hands and fingers over the scars, the ugly reminders of a brutal childhood. "I wish I could erase them with my fingertips. I wish I could erase all of it for you."

"You are, baby."

TWENTY-ONE
COLT

With no covers on the windows, the morning sun poked its head through the glass like an annoying, nosy neighbor. I turned over to find that Jade wasn't next to me. I sat up with a start.

She walked out of the kitchen with a cup of coffee and her new hair color. "I'm getting used to the brunette look," I said. "Of course, you could have a shaved head and you'd still be hot."

"I think I'll stick with the new color. A shaved head sounds cold." She'd pulled on one of my t-shirts. She glanced down at it. "Hope you don't mind. I've grown very fond of wearing your shirts."

"I love when you wear my shirts. Now get your cute ass over here, so I can take it off of you."

"Actually . . ." She smiled and yanked out one of the

fabric strips I'd used last night to tie her up. "I had another idea."

"Fuck yeah. You want to be tied up again, darlin'. I'm all for it. Now get back into this bed."

She walked over swinging the fabric piece around in circles. She stepped onto the mattress, and I reached for the strip of cloth. She held it up out of my grasp. "Nope. It's my turn."

She straddled me, took hold of my hands and put them up above my head. She bit her lip as she struggled to tie them together. It was fucking cute to watch, and it was making my cock stand straight up, especially with her pussy rubbing against me.

"You realize I could probably rip that strip of cloth with one pull," I said.

She sat back with a satisfied smile. "I know," she said confidently. "But, if you do, I'll stop my plans, and—" She scooted back and knelt between my legs. Her hand wrapped around my cock and she moved it up and down the shaft, making sure to rub her thumb in the liquid pooling at the tip. "I don't think you're going to want me to stop." She leaned down and licked the same liquid just before taking my cock in her mouth. She lowered her lips down, taking in as much as she could. Her mouth tightened around me. I lifted my tied hands and tangled them in her hair. I held her head over me as she moved up and down my cock, coaxing even more pre-cum from me. One of her small hands held the base of my cock while the other fondled my balls. I tightened my ass and pushed farther into her mouth. Her tongue slid over me.

"Fuck, baby, I'm going to come, but I want to be inside of you."

I ripped the fabric strip. She looked up stunned.

"I warned you." I reached forward and pulled her toward me. "Now drop that pussy of yours over me right now.

She giggled wildly as I grabbed her hips and positioned her over my cock. Her laughter faded, and she closed her eyes as she lowered herself over me. She braced her hands on my chest and rocked her body against me.

Even though we'd gone at it all night long, the two of us were so completely turned on by each other, so damn connected, we both came almost instantly.

I reached up, and she pressed my hand against her face.

"Do you think it's possible we'll ever get bored of this?" she asked.

"Not a chance." I looked up at her. "I don't see myself ever being without you, Jade. Our boat was sitting on that dock for a reason. It was meant to be there to carry you home, to me."

She climbed off of me and stretched out next to me,

resting her head on my chest. I placed my arm around her. "It sure is quiet here," she said.

"The highway is just far enough away that you can't hear any traffic except for the occasional truck horn. If you listen really carefully though, you can hear the ocean rolling in. I think that calmness was what brought my brothers and me here a lot. That and Noddy's cookies, of course." I thought about those afternoons when we'd ride over here on our crummy bikes. Mine always had a flat tire, but I pumped it along behind Hunter and Slade. We knew we'd get here, and for that short period of time, we'd live without fear and the uncertainty my dad's temper brought with every new day. For that short span of time, we were no longer the rowdy, out of control, severely neglected Stone brothers. We left all the ugly shit behind when we stepped through Noddy's front door.

"I'm glad you had her," Jade said. "And, with how quiet and remote it is out here, I'm glad she had you boys."

"Yep, occasionally you just get lucky in the people part of your life." I squeezed her against me. Sometimes I wanted her so badly I worried that I would crush her.

Jade pointed to a place on the wall where I'd painted on three color samples. "That's interesting."

"I was trying to decide on a color."

She laughed.

"I know, it looks funny."

"No, I'm just picturing you tapping your chin and trying to decide on a color. You're not exactly the interior decorator type."

"Hey, I have a sensitive side. I appreciate beauty." I reached down and spanked her once. "As you may have noticed."

"I guess every hard exterior has a soft core."

"I know you've landed right on my soft core. I don't think anyone has ever come close to finding it."

She looked up at me and kissed my chin. "Ouch." She rubbed her lips. "I've also found your less than soft beard stubble." She relaxed her head against my chest and stared up at the paint samples. "The pale teal color," she said. "I think that's the one Noddy would have picked."

"Then that's the color I'll use." My phone buzzed. I reached to the floor and picked it up. "Hey, Street, what's up? By the way, I got Jade a phone, I'll have her call you to give you the number."

"Oh good. I was afraid I wasn't going to get to talk to her. Figured you were going to keep her all to yourself."

"Damn right I'm keeping her to myself. What's new? Did you guys yank those flyers?"

"Yeah, think we got most of them." There was a knock on the door. Jade startled. I placed my finger against my mouth to tell her to keep quiet, and I grabbed my jeans off the floor. I stuck the phone in between my shoulder and ear and pulled the pants on.

"Hey, Street, got to call you back. There's someone at my door." I glanced around looking for something to swing that would dent a skull.

"I know there's someone at your door, dork. It's me. Now, open up before I spill the coffees."

Jade was standing with her arms crossed around herself looking pale and shaken.

"It's just Amy."

She smiled with relief.

I swung open the door. "Fuck, Street, I was just about to grab a chair to clobber you with."

"Real nice greeting for the breakfast delivery girl." She swept in past me with a tray of coffees and a white bag.

I glanced out to the yard and the long gravel road that led to the cottage. It was deserted.

The girls took the coffees into the kitchen where I'd set up a rickety coffee table and some old boxes.

I grabbed my cup of coffee. "You've got to be careful coming out here, Street. We're trying not to draw attention to this place."

She broke off a piece of pastry and licked her finger. "Too late. You two, it turns out, have already been drawing attention all over town. I mean the town bad boy and heartthrob hanging out with the new, pretty stranger— it's the stuff for tabloid headlines. Can't make that shit up."

"Actually, I think most of those headlines are made up," Jade noted. The color had returned to her cheeks as she sipped her coffee.

"Shit, do you mean there really isn't a boy who is half human and half bat? Those pictures were so convincing." Street shoved another bite of pastry between her lips and drank it down with some coffee. "Anyhow, everyone knows Jade is the girl on the flyer and that she's hanging with you. But here's the kicker— Hunter was up the coast at the pool hall." She rolled her eyes. "He said he was going up there to trash the flyers, but I saw right through his excuse. He's hot on the trail of a new bartender up there." She twisted her mouth, and her expression softened. "Asshole," she muttered under her breath. "Anyhow, he dragged his sorry ass in after midnight. I fell asleep on the couch." She pointed a finger at me. "But I wasn't waiting for him, so don't say a fucking thing, Colt."

I lifted my hands in surrender. "Didn't say a damn word."

She sighed. "My mom's been talking in her sleep like crazy, and I'm about to go nuts. So, I crashed on the couch. Slade came in right after him, and Hunter was telling him that the asshole you guys keep meeting out on the water was there asking questions about Jade."

"You mean Ace?"

"Didn't hear a name. He told Slade 'the motherfucker who likes to shove his gun at Colt's head.' I've got somewhat of an idea of what you *fishermen* are doing out there on the water but sounds like you guys need to shift professions."

Jade was looking at the side of my face, but I didn't want to talk to her about any of it right now. "He likes to shove his gun at you?" she asked.

I shook my head. "It's nothing. It's just how he does things, but I'm more worried about what he's up to. He wants that reward money, and I'm sure there are plenty of others with the same plan."

Jade didn't look too satisfied with my answer, but I wasn't about to get into details about our drug running business. I was sure it wouldn't score me points with her. I grabbed up a pastry. "Since I'm out here I'm going to do some patching on the roof so the house is ready for the next rainstorm. I'll leave you two to your breakfast."

TWENTY-TWO
JADE

Amy and I watched as Colt walked out the door in his tool belt and work boots. In an impromptu role reversal, women whistling at the construction hottie, we both made impressive attempts at a catcall. Colt stopped in the kitchen doorway and wiggled his ass before walking outside.

The door had barely shut when Amy reached over and took my hand. "Oh my god, I've never seen him like this. That boy is smitten, crushing, batshit crazy, whatever the hell you want to call it. How does it feel?"

I picked off a piece of pastry. "How does what feel?"

"To break through that stone exterior. Shit, you're the first girl to ever do so. Many have tried, believe me. I've even had girls become my best friend"—her air quotes followed—"just to get close to Colt." She sighed and sat back. "Wish I knew your secret. I had that date with Brock, the beer delivery guy. All I could think about was that stupid giant, Hunter. And he's so fucking rotten to me all the time."

I pressed my hand over hers. "Amy, when you're not looking, that man is keeping a close eye on you. Colt told me no other local guys would get near you because they're afraid of Hunter. That shows how much he cares about you."

"Yeah, sort of like having the plague. No one will get near me, but at the same time Hunter treats me like an annoying pest most of the time."

"Then maybe you need to be the ice queen for awhile. Show him that he takes you for granted too much."

She seemed to be mulling over my words. "I might try that. Brock asked me on a second date, but I haven't decided. Maybe I'll give it another chance."

"Good idea."

Amy's phone buzzed, and she pulled it out of her pocket. She groaned with frustration as she answered. "Hey, Mom."

She rolled her eyes and swirled her finger around by her temple. I felt bad for her having to deal with her mom's health all by herself. It couldn't be easy. "No one sprayed poison on the bananas, Mom. Just eat one. You'll be fine." Her brows creased together, and she shook her head. "All right. I'll come home right now and make you a breakfast that hasn't been tainted by poison." She put the phone in her pocket. "Good times, huh? I'm living with a crazy woman, and you've got a crazy man offering a bounty to find you. But, at least you have Colt. I've got no one."

"That's not true. You've got me, and I love having you as a friend, Amy."

She reached over and hugged me. "You're right. Enough of my pity party. I've got to go home and save my mom from the tiny green men who are lacing her fruit with cyanide. Now that you have a phone, we can talk anytime. I'll call you later."

I walked her out and sat on the small fence surrounding the backyard. Colt was up on the roof with a roll of black paper. Some of the shingles had been removed. They were stacked next to him.

"Where's Amy heading?" he called down.

"Her mom thought someone put poison in the bananas."

He shook his head. "Amy has the patience of a fucking saint."

"Yeah, and not just with her mom."

He glanced down at me. "What do you mean?"

"What the heck is the deal with Hunter?"

"Oh, that. Not sure. I never really know what's going on in my brother's head, but I can tell you, if Amy found someone else, he'd feel it like a kick in the gut." He hammered down some of the black material. "Speaking of Hunter— he texted that he needs some help at the boat. He's been working on the engine, and he needs another pair of hands." He looked over the edge. "I was hoping Amy was sticking around a little longer. Do you think you'll be all right alone for a few hours?"

"I'm sure I can manage. I was going to look through some of those old dusty boxes. Noddy had some cool stuff."

"Good idea. And when I come back, I'll start a fire." He lifted a brow. "I'm looking for a complete repeat of last night."

"A repeat?"

"Well, maybe I'll mix it up a little to surprise you."

TWENTY-THREE
COLT

Hunter's motorcycle wasn't parked in its usual spot by the docks, which was not completely unusual, especially since his bike had been having problems. Still, I couldn't remember the last time Hunter had made the trek to the boat on foot. He'd ride his damn bike down the hallway to his room if the handlebars weren't too wide. I checked my phone. He hadn't texted me since the last message asking me to meet him on the *Durango* at noon.

I decided to check and see if Jade was keeping her phone near her. I sent her a quick text. "Miss you already. Everything all right?" Most of the boats were still out fishing, the only other signs of life were a few pelicans waiting for the fishing boats to return. Aside from the *Durango*, only a few other vessels bobbed up and down in the water.

There was no sign of Hunter as I neared the boat. Jade texted back. I stopped to read it.

"Everything is good. I guess no gas means no hot water either. I took a speedy shower, but now I'm in desperate need of body heat. Only yours will do."

"Damn, I better get back quick then." A call from Slade came through, and I answered it. "What's up and where's Hunter?"

"His lazy ass is still in bed. Think he spent the evening fucking that new drink server up north."

"That idiot. He texted me an hour ago to meet him at the *Durango*."

"Nah, couldn't be. He came home last night complaining that someone had jacked his phone out of his coat pocket while he was playing a round of pool. But I was calling to tell you that this black car keeps driving by the house."

"Wait." I scrolled through to the text. It was from Hunter's phone. "He must have found it because the text came from him. What car?" Footsteps pounded the wood planks behind me. Before I could turn around, the hard end of gun barrel pressed against my back. I sensed there were at least three men standing behind me, including the one with the gun jammed into my kidney.

"Fuck."

"What's wrong?" Slade asked.

A hand reached forward and grabbed the phone away. The guy patted me down, but I wasn't carrying a gun. I hadn't needed one for helping Hunter with the boat.

"We're just going to walk real slow to the boat at the end of the dock," the unfamiliar voice said.

I turned my head and glimpsed his two partners. I didn't recognize any of them, but something told me they were part of Ward's new security team. One of the guys had a skull tattooed on the side of his neck. He looked like the kind that finished his beer by chewing up the can. One looked as if he ate steroids for breakfast. He'd stretched an extremely small black shirt over his shoulders to accentuate his arms.

I shot him an amused smile.

"You're on the wrong end of a gun to be grinning like that, boy," he snarled.

Whenever I was in trouble, I always managed to dig myself deeper with my big mouth, and I figured I might as well keep the tradition going. "No, man, you're right. I was just wondering though— do you need an extension on your comb to be able to reach your head with those big, beefy arms? In fact, how the hell do manage to wipe your ass? Or maybe you don't."

His thick fingers pinched my skin as he grabbed my shirt. He brought his ugly horse face right up to mine.

"You smart ass, I'm going to have fun messing up that face of yours."

"Never mind," I said. "You answered my second question. Your breath smells like shit."

The guy with the gun in my back shoved it hard into my muscle, and I stumbled forward. Muscleman took the opportunity to throw his fist into my stomach. I coughed and sucked in the salty air hovering over the dock.

The gunman pressed his weapon against my back again. "Enough of the smartass shit. Keep moving or I'll shoot you dead here and toss you over the side."

I walked toward their boat. It was a nice ski boat, but something told me these guys didn't do many water sports. "Great. Are we going to do some wakeboarding?" I asked.

Muscleman, who had obviously taken an instant disliking to me, kicked me hard. I flew over the side and onto the deck. He hopped into the boat next to me. The entire vessel tilted to the side with his weight.

I got a good look at the gunman too. He was smaller than the other two and looked a bit more brainy. "Don't give us any ideas, Stone," he said. "Otherwise, I might just tie you to a tow line and drag you across the fucking water."

"So, you know my name is Stone, and I guess there's a purpose to this whole fucking thing. But something tells me this isn't one of those crazy fun birthday kidnappings where you drag me blindfolded into a strip joint and have some nice girl give me a lap dance."

"Tie him up good and cover his fucking mouth. I can't listen to his bullshit anymore," the gunman sneered.

"So, that's a no on the strip club?" I asked.

The one guy had the muscles, but it turned out the dude with the skull tattoo had the right hook. His fist slammed my chin, and my teeth clamped down hard on my tongue. Blood oozed toward my throat. I spit a nice red loogie onto the polished wood deck.

Muscleman grabbed my hands and tied them with rope. His friend tied up my feet. Then, with a great amount of pleasure, muscleman stuffed a dirty rag into my bloody mouth.

I sat back against the bench and began trying to work loose my hands. But there was a solid knot in the rope. We took off going south. I watched the three men. They said nothing to each other as the boat coasted out to sea, slowly at first, and then gaining speed once we were past the buoys. The rag they'd stuffed in my mouth was pungent with some kind of cleaner, but it helped to absorb the blood dripping off my tongue. There was no doubt in my mind that Ward had sent these guys. Word had gotten around that Jade was with me. Most people in the area knew me, so I was easy to find.

Whatever the hell it was on the cloth, varnish or paint thinner or some other pungent shit, it was giving me an unwanted buzz. I needed to keep my head clear. I wasn't completely sure what they had planned for me, but I didn't want to be high on fumes when it went down. My jaw was numb from the hit as I moved it to work the cloth forward. I spit the gag out and a fine shower of spit and blood came with it. Muscleman and skull stared down at the blood soaked cloth. Neither, it seemed, were inclined to touch it. I decided to just keep my mouth shut and keep an eye on where we were headed.

The boat slammed over the choppy water, and I bounced on the bench. Being tied up made it hard to keep balanced, and twice, my head slammed the railing behind me. Slade had mentioned a black car driving by the house. My biggest worry was that someone had followed Amy to the cottage. Jade was all alone out there. Slade knew something was up, and he knew I was at the boat when I was talking to him. But it was impossible to follow a trail on the water, especially when you didn't know which boat to follow. This bookie was going to some extraordinary lengths to get Jade back, and I couldn't blame the guy. She wasn't a girl you could easily watch walk away. Almost felt sorry for the fucker. Of course, I also wanted to pound him into pulp.

After a rough trip over the water at top speed, we

pulled up to a private dock. A big stone and wood cabin loomed above on a small bluff behind the beach. It looked like a rich man's beach house, Ward's no doubt. We pulled up to the dock and gunman and skull tied off the boat.

I decided to keep my mouth shut and keep an eye out for a chance to get away. My first chance came when muscleman untied my feet. My hands were still secured behind my back. He gave me a boost up to the dock. The second my feet hit solid wood planks, I spun around and kicked him hard in the face. He flew back onto the deck of the boat, landing solidly on the engine compartment. I took off at a run, but skull tackled me hard. With no hands to stop me, my face slammed against the dock. My head buzzed as if my brain was vibrating from the impact.

Muscleman had recovered from the kick, but his face was red from my boot mark and from rage. He and skull yanked me to my feet and walked me toward the house. Then we veered left, and they took me up a long path to a waiting van. The door slid open and a new face, a man with red hair and a red beard, peered out. He had a gun too. He pointed it directly at my face. Ward had a big fucking crew.

Muscleman, who was still pissed as hell about the kick, shoved me so hard into the van my head whipped back. I fell face first into the cargo hold. The door slid shut. Red kept a gun on me while the others climbed into the front of the van. We were off. There were no windows, and I had no fucking clue where I was headed, but something told me the next face I saw would be the man himself.

I propped myself up. I moved slowly because red seemed extra nervous and possibly a little trigger happy. He never lowered the gun but kept it trained on me like I was a rattler poised to strike at any second.

I leaned my head back against the metal wall of the van and closed my eyes. The face slam on the dock had given me a headache. Every movement of my jaw sent shooting pain through my face. Something told me this was only the beginning. I hadn't personally ever dealt with Ward. Gambling was more Hunter's thing. From what he'd told me, the man was ruthless when someone didn't pay up in time. I guess you don't get awesome beach houses and a loyal army of thugs unless you're cutthroat. I would most likely end up dead once this was over, but I wasn't going out without a fight. I was going to do everything I could to keep the asshole away from Jade. It would figure that the one time I let my guard down with a girl she'd have all kinds of shitty baggage behind her.

TWENTY-FOUR
JADE

I paced back and forth from the mattress to the pile of Noddy's things in the corner. I'd sent a text back asking how long Colt would be, and there was no response. Slade had called me right after to see if I'd seen Colt. He said that they'd been talking. Then some other voices came through the phone, and Colt had stopped responding. Hunter had confirmed that he definitely hadn't sent any text to Colt about meeting him at the boat.

I waited anxiously to hear from Slade and Hunter. They were driving to the dock to check out the boat and ask around to see if anyone had seen Colt.

A knock at the door made me stiffen but then Amy called to me. "It's me, Jade. Let me in."

I ran to the door. "Any word?"

Amy looked just as worried as I felt. She shook her head and hugged me. "But Slade and Hunter will find him. Besides, Colt is a badass. He can definitely take care of himself. Have you seen anyone out here yet? Slade said some guys kept driving by the house earlier. Do you think it's that guy who's looking for you? I mean the boys are always dealing with some sketchy shit, but none of it has ever come to their doorstep."

I swallowed to alleviate the dryness in my throat. "This was the last thing I wanted to happen. I should have just left town. Now I've put Colt and all of you in danger." My voice shook with despair.

"Don't fall apart now. We need you to keep your wits about you. You might have to lead the boys to this guy's house." She put her arm around my shoulder and led me to the kitchen. We sat down.

"That's where we should be heading right now," I said.

"The guys are just talking to the fishermen and other boat owners. I guess there was a pleasure boat or something parked near the *Durango* this morning, and no one knew who it belonged to. We'll wait for their call."

TWENTY-FIVE
COLT

The steady vibration of the van and the drowsy feeling that was swarming my aching head, nearly made me fall asleep. I didn't need to be a doctor to know that I'd gotten a concussion when I face planted on the dock. I'd had more than my share of them. In fact, sometimes I wondered how much of my brain was pudding because of it. I was half asleep and nearly pitched sideways when the van came to a stop.

The driver and passenger doors opened and shut, and the cargo door slid open. The light poured in causing a searing pain in my head. I was yanked from the van and into an empty parking lot that was more weeds than asphalt. I looked around but couldn't pinpoint where we were. We were definitely inland. The air was warmer, and there was no ocean breeze.

The building in the lot seemed to be in the middle of an abandoned industrial park, possibly some developer's big plan gone sour.

Skull took me by the arm. My new buddies and I headed toward the abandoned building. The interior was just as I'd expected, dark cement floor, bare cinderblock walls and some hanging wire dangling from a mosaic of steel girders crisscrossing the room.

Gunman was on the phone the second they pulled the heavy drop down door shut behind us. Since the building was like a big empty cave, it was easy to hear his conversation. Not that he was trying to hide it. I was pretty sure I knew who was on the other end.

"Yeah, we've got him. All right. See you in a few."

Gunman motioned up to the metal railing. "Secure him," he ordered. I was outnumbered and armed with nothing but my strength and wits, both of which had been dulled by the swishing in my head. My vision was definitely blurry. I'd taken a harder knock than I realized. My arms were yanked up as skull threw the end of the rope over one of the steel girders. The loose end was tied to the knot around my wrists. It only took a few seconds before my hands began to tingle with numbness. Even with my legs free, I had no real way to defend myself.

Muscleman sneered up at me. "You're not such a

wiseass now that you're strung up like a pig about to be gutted."

I stared down at him. "Guess now you figure it's a fair fight, eh, you thick-necked clown. It's four against one, not including the hardware you dicks have shoved under your shirts. Yet you still felt the need to string me up. Cowards."

He shrugged and turned away. Then he spun back around. He pummeled me like a fucking punching bag. Every blow hurt like hell and forced the wind from me. Through the flurry of punches, I heard the door to the building open. Muscleman stopped.

Ward stepped into view. He sauntered in like the king of the world. I half expected his crew to bow to him.

He stopped in front of me but out of kicking range. I badly wanted to throw a foot at his smirking face. "So, you're Colt Stone. Guess you and I have something very important in common."

"I don't think so," I grunted, still trying to pull back in the air that muscleman had pounded out of me. Every breath hurt enough to take my mind off the sizzling pain in my head.

"Really? And why is that?" Ward asked.

I was already pissed as hell but looking at this fucker and thinking about the marks he'd left on Jade was making my blood boil. "Because you had to drag her to your bed kicking and screaming. She climbs into mine with a smile."

He stared up at me without blinking, but a tiny twitch in his jaw assured me I'd gotten to him. It was my only line of defense. It was probably going to bring me a lot more pain, but it was still satisfying.

Ward looked at the gunman. "Do you have the phone?"

The man pulled my phone out of his pocket. Ward swiped his thumb over the screen and smiled. "Ah, clever, you didn't want to put her name on it. *The One.* How fucking cute is that? But she will be coming back to me soon, so I hope you said your farewells."

"There's no fucking way she's going back to you. You can do whatever the fuck you'd like to me, I'm not telling you where she is. You should just move on and leave her alone, you goddamn psycho."

"Can't do that. Besides, I'm not counting on you to tell me a thing. My informant, the fool who thinks he's in line for ten grand, told me you were like your name, a fucking stone." He read Jade's last text and held up the phone. "She wants to know how long you'll be. What should I tell her? Wait." He moved his fingers over the phone and pressed send. "I told her you were going to be awhile because we were beating the shit out of you." He held the phone on his palm and tossed it up and down once.

Ward looked around at his men. "Don't know what the hell you're waiting for. Mess him up good, and keep out of the way so I can get some good shots." He grinned at me. "See, I know Jade a lot better than you. That's how I know she'll be back with me soon. I don't have to find her. She'll come to me."

Muscle was the first to take a shot. His fist plowed into my face, and once again, my jaw clamped painfully shut. My lip split and blood trickled from the cut. Skull man came up next. He worried me more. He had just enough muscle to make his shots more effective than his overstuffed friend.

Ward lifted the phone to get a picture of skull pounding me in the gut. I felt some ribs give way as I sucked the air to try and get a breath. He followed with a fist to my face. Blackness followed the explosion of pain.

TWENTY-SIX

JADE

Amy and I sat feeling utterly helpless and distraught. I knew Ray was ruthless, but I wasn't sure if he was capable of cold blooded murder. That last night on the dock, when he'd grabbed my throat, it seemed that he would have killed me if I hadn't kicked him. But that had been provoked by passion and rage. This was different. He didn't even know Colt.

Amy's phone buzzed. She read the text. "Slade and Hunter have a lead on the boat. Someone recognized it as a boat that is always moored off a private dock on Lander's Beach."

"That's Ray's beach house. It must have been his ski boat. I know the address of the beach house if that will help."

Amy texted them back and sent them the address.

She got up from the table. "I've got to take a pee. Remember, don't open for anyone. Even if Charlie friggin' Hunnam shows up on his Harley with his hot little white sneakers, don't open the damn door."

I smiled. "That's asking a lot, but I'll ignore him." She was just about out of the kitchen. "Amy, thanks for staying here with me."

"Of course." She headed toward the bathroom.

I still wasn't used to the sound of my phone, and it startled me at first. I picked it up. My heart nearly leapt into my throat. It was a text from Colt. "Lover boy is going to be awhile because my guys are beating the shit out of him." My hands shook as I stared in disbelief at the screen. It beeped again. It took me a few seconds to work up the courage to look at the picture. A sob bubbled from my mouth, and I stifled the next one with my hand. A man with massive arms was throwing his fist into Colt's face. Colt's shirt and face were covered in blood, and his hands were tied up above his head.

My fingers shook so badly, it was nearly impossible to touch the keypad. I dialed Colt's phone. It only took one ring. The sound of Ray's voice made a bitter taste rise in my throat. "Hello, sweetheart, I figured you'd be calling soon. Your sparkling new lover ain't looking so hot anymore. Boys, throw that water at him. I want him conscious."

"You monster, I'll see that you go to jail for life," I

cried. Amy came into the kitchen with a questioning look on her face. I nodded. Tears clouded my vision, and I took a long steadying breath. I heard water splashing and a groan of pain that I knew came from Colt. I bit my lip to keep from breaking into sobs. "What do you want? I'll do anything."

"See, now that's cooperation. All I want is you to come back to me, and I'll let Stone go. I'll text you the location. I've got men all around the lot, so if you show up with anyone else or if there's anyone following you, then he dies. Simple as that."

"Send me the address. I'm coming right now." I took a deep breath. "And don't touch him anymore, you bastard!"

Amy sat down. Tears streamed down her cheeks. "What's happening? Is Colt all right?"

I handed her the phone. She stared at the picture and despair turned to anger. "I'm sending this to Hunter. He's going to tear that man to pieces."

I took the phone from her. "No, you can't. I have to show up alone or he'll kill Colt." I pressed my hand against my stomach to keep from throwing up. Just thinking about the picture and the idea that Colt might die because of me made me sick with anguish. "I need to borrow your car, Amy."

"Yes, sure, but I'm coming with you."

"You can't. Slade and Hunter can't show up either,

or they'll kill him. I have no doubt Ray will make good on his threat. I brought this on. I'm just going to head back to Ray. I'll figure a way to get free of him eventually, but for now, all I care about is freeing Colt."

"I don't know, Jade. Maybe I could hide in the backseat."

"Then you'd be at risk too. Please, Amy, just lend me the car."

She pulled out her keys and handed them to me. "Colt is going to kill me for letting you go alone."

"I'll be fine. But I need to get there fast. Colt looks really bad." Another cry shook me.

Amy gave me a quick hug. "Be careful."

I raced outside. Amy watched from the porch as I started her car and took off down the unpaved road. Ray had texted the address right after I hung up with him. I knew the building. He'd purchased it six months earlier as an investment, but it had been a real estate deal gone bad. And he'd been plenty pissed about it too. Now, it seemed, he'd found a sinister use for the empty warehouse.

A twenty minute drive felt like an hour. My hands were trembling, and I still felt close to puking. I had to pull myself together. I needed to be the negotiator and actress. I had to convince Ray that I was willing to be back with him as long as I saw Colt released.

The parking lot had decayed even more. Tall weeds

stuck out between the large fissures in the broken mosaic of asphalt. I turned into the deserted lot and drove to the back toward the empty warehouse. Ray's Mercedes and a white van were parked outside the building. Two of his men, guys I didn't recognize, were standing like sentries outside. They both kept a hand on the guns in their shoulder holsters as I stepped out of the car.

I held up my hands. "I'm alone."

One of them opened the door for me, and I stepped inside. A small cry chirped from my lips as I caught sight of Colt standing in the center of the vast, empty room. His face was a mixture of pale white, black bruises and red blood. He had a hard time focusing as he lifted his head. I couldn't stop myself.

I ran past Ray and the sadistic assholes who had been beating him and threw my arms around him. "I'm so sorry. This is my fault." They'd soaked him with cold water, and his strong body was shivering in my embrace.

"Damnit, baby, why'd you come? You should have stayed away."

I peered up. He was looking down at me through swollen lids. His lip was split open and a red stream of blood trickled from the gash and ran down his chin to his neck and shirt.

"This is very fucking touching," Ray sneered from

behind me. I hadn't looked at his face yet, and I had to brace myself to do it. I turned to him.

His dark eyes flickered with the same hatred I was feeling. "Not sure how I feel about the new hair color, but I guess we can change that back now that you're out of hiding."

"Release him right now, and we can go home. I'll do anything you ask, but let him go."

I turned back to Colt. "I have Amy's car. Can you drive?"

"Not leaving without you."

"Yes, you have to." I hugged him again. "I'll get away from him again," I whispered. I looked up at his bloodied and bruised face. "I need someone to run to once I get free." My throat tightened as I said the words. The truth was I didn't think I'd ever be free of Ray. He would kill me first. I was certain of it.

"Let's be on our way then, Jade," Ray said.

"I want to see him freed first."

"Cut him down."

One of the men reached up with a sharp blade and cut through the rope. Colt collapsed. I caught him but my legs buckled under his weight. Two of the men grabbed his arms to prop him upright.

"Don't do this, Jade." Colt's voice was low and gritty.

I pressed my hand gently against his face. Blood

covered my palm as I kissed the side of his mouth that wasn't cut. I stuck the car keys in his pocket. "I will find a way back to you," I said quietly.

"No need," Colt grunted. "I'm coming for you, so you wait. Do you understand, baby? You fucking wait for me."

Ray walked over and wrenched my arm painfully.

Colt's face reddened with anger. "I'm going to kill you, motherfucker. You're a fucking dead man."

Ray laughed. It was a sound that had always made me cringe. He dragged me toward the door. I stumbled reluctantly behind him. "What about him? I want to see him get in the car."

Ray's sharp whistle made me jump. "Bring the piece of garbage out to the parking lot."

I glanced back. They held Colt up and made their way to the door. Ray's fingers cut off the circulation in my arm like a tourniquet as he yanked me along to his car. I craned my neck to see what was happening with Colt.

They walked toward Amy's car. Ray opened the door on the Mercedes and shoved me into the front seat. I kept my face glued to the window. Colt's green gaze caught mine, and we stared at each other long and hard. The men were still holding him next to Amy's car when Ray climbed into the driver's seat. He started the engine.

"Why aren't they letting him get in the car?" I asked frantically.

Ray didn't answer. He circled the Mercedes around. The men pulled Colt back toward the white van.

"No!" I screamed. I grabbed the door handle, and it flew open as the car circled around. Ray grabbed my arm so hard, sharp pain shot up to my shoulder. He pulled me roughly into the seat and turned the wheel sharply so that the door slammed shut again.

"You were supposed to let him go!" I screamed.

Ray laughed. "Gullible little bitch."

I threw a fist at his head. The car swerved into a trash bin, putting a gash in the side of his precious Mercedes. He returned the favor. His big, heavy hand came across and backhanded me so hard, I blacked out.

TWENTY-SEVEN
COLT

I leaned up against the side of the van and took several deep, steadying breaths. I'd figured all along that I was a dead man. I just didn't want to let Jade know. Now he had her. My teeth gritted in anger causing my jaw to throb with pain.

Red sat at the front end of the cargo hold with the gun held loosely in his hand. He'd apparently decided I was messed up enough to not put up a fight. They had tossed me inside the van without bothering to tie up my hands again. My head and body felt like shit, and I wasn't sure if I could fight back. I closed my eyes to try and calm the pain messing with my mind. I needed to think clearly and get past all the bruises, cuts and broken bones. I planned to go out with a big fucking fight. Jade needed me more than ever now. I needed to get out of this for no other reason except to save her.

The van was moving along at a good pace. From the drop in temperature inside the van, it seemed we were heading back toward the water. I glanced over at Red. "We're heading back to the boat, huh? It's really nice of you guys to give me a ride back to my hometown dock. Don't think I'd be able to make the swim with the way I'm feeling."

"Yeah, you'll be taking a swim all right."

That was the plan. I'd gotten the fool to tell me without even asking. They were going to take me out on the water, shoot me and drop me into the ocean. My only chance was to grab red's gun, but with the way we sat at the moment, there was no chance. He'd be able to shoot me in the face long before I made a grab for the gun. I needed to wait for the right opportunity.

The van veered right and slowed. We were leaving the highway. It was just a few miles to the private dock where they'd moored the boat. My body felt as if it had been through the fucking wringer. Working up any adrenaline to make my move was harder than I'd expected. But something told me, when the chance presented itself, I'd move into action.

We made several right turns. The van was getting closer to the beach house. A sharp turn and a bump told me we were traveling on the long path to the water. Then the van came to a sudden violent stop as if it had hit something. The voices were muffled by the dividing wall between the cargo hold and the cab of the van, but they grew louder. The driver and passenger doors opened.

Red got up and hunched over as he reached to slide open the door. I kicked his feet out from under him, and he hit the floor elbow first. The gun fell from his grip. I snatched it and held it against his forehead.

He scowled up at me.

I motioned with my head toward the door. "Slide it open."

As he opened the door, skull went flying past the opening, landing hard on the driveway. I shoved red out with my foot and climbed out with my gun, ready to kill any fucker who came near me.

Slade's grinning face greeted me. "Holy shit, you're a mess."

Loud grunts came from the other side of the van. Slade leaned his head that direction. "Hunter is taking care of the circus strongman back there."

A low groan came from behind me. Skull was just coming to. Slade had already done a number on him. He pushed halfway to his feet. Slade stepped forward, but I put up a hand to stop him.

"My turn." My leg flew out. I kicked the guy's head so hard, blood flew from his ears. He flopped face down on the driveway. I looked around. "Where's the fourth guy?"

"The small dude ran toward the beach. Hunter scared him."

Hunter walked around to our side of the van. His knuckles were bright red, and there was some blood sprayed on his shirt. But it wasn't his blood. "Who did I scare?" He looked at me. "Fuck. What the hell did they do, drag you behind a fucking horse?"

"Feels like it. We've got to get back—" A gunshot fired through the trees, and we all ducked. Slade reached for his gun.

"I've got this. I'm suddenly feeling much better, and I'm in the mood for a little payback." I headed to a small brick wall that lined the driveway and dropped down behind it. I waited for a flicker of movement. There was more than a flicker. Another shot was fired. He was just shooting blindly. I, on the other hand, saw exactly where the shot had come from. The second he dashed away from the tree he'd been hiding behind, I fired a round. He yelled out and grabbed his leg.

Hunter nodded. "Not bad for a guy who looks like he's been run over by a tractor."

"Let's get out of here. We need to get to Ward's place and find Jade. She's in a lot of danger."

"Yep, we've got the address," Slade said. "That was

where we were headed after this place if we couldn't find you."

Hunter walked over and patted me on the shoulder. "Glad we found you, little bro."

"Yeah, me too."

TWENTY-EIGHT
JADE

I came to just as Ray was pulling into the driveway. For a second, the facade of the house looked so familiar, I'd forgotten what had happened. For a split second of time, I was back with Ray still trying to figure out how to eventually free myself from the man I hated. Then Colt's battered face flashed through my mind, and I broke into sobs.

Ray walked around to the passenger side and gripped my arm like a vise as he pulled me roughly from the car. "You'll have to get over this drama scene fast, sweetheart, because it's getting on my nerves."

"You were supposed to let him go," I cried. "That was part of the deal." I wrenched my arm free and ran. He grabbed my hair. I reached back to keep him from ripping it out of my head. I fell back hard on my ass, but he kept his grip on my hair. He yanked on it, and I reached up to the roots to stop the pain.

"Get up or I'll drag you back to the house by your hair."

I got to my feet. My tailbone ached from the fall. I sighed with relief when he released my hair. His hand wrapped around my wrist. There were several men standing in front of the house like guards.

"See, you're so fucking hated, you have to pay people to protect you from your enemies."

"That's what happens when you make a lot of money." We got to the front door. "Seems you can buy anything when you have big bucks." He opened the door and pushed me inside. "By now, that scumbag you were living with is dead. If you leave, there'll be no one to run to. Besides, I'll just track you down again."

I swayed on my feet. I'd caused Colt's death. The man I loved. I thought about that for a second. I loved him. It wasn't just passion and an infatuation, I had fallen in love with Colt.

I spun around. "Then just kill me. Living here with you is far worse than a long, slow death."

"That can be arranged too. Don't bother to run. The guards are there to keep enemies out and you in." He walked toward his study, which, of course, meant he was going for the bourbon. In less than an hour, he'd be drunk and even more vile.

I watched him walk to his study door and realized my hatred for the man had gone past the point of sanity. He'd killed Colt for no reason. I grabbed a heavy copper vase from the table in the entry. I ran toward Ray. The fake flowers fluttered to the ground as I lifted the vase over my head.

Ray turned around and lifted his arm. My forearms nearly broke in half as they smacked his hard arm. The vase bounced off his shoulder and clanged loudly as it clattered to the marble floor. He swung his fist at me, and I stumbled back. Shards of light sparked across my vision and I couldn't tell which way was up. I fell hard onto the cold floor.

Ray reached down and pinched my skin painfully as he grabbed my arm. This time, he didn't wait for me to get to my feet. The skin on my legs stuttered along the smooth floor as he dragged me to his study. My head lolled back as he grabbed both my arms and jerked me to my feet. With a solid push, he shoved me onto the sofa. My neck snapped and my head jolted back and forth. Everything turned fuzzy gray. I flopped down on the cushions and hid my face to keep the room from spinning.

Through the haze, I heard Ray unlock his liquor cabinet. My mind drifted in and out of reality. One minute, I was leaned over his desk trying to plunge a letter opener into his face, and the next, I was safe and secure in Colt's arms. That vision and the reality that I'd lost Colt forever made me curl into a ball of quiet hysteria. Now, my only hope was that Ray would get drunk enough to kill me. I wanted the end to come soon so that I didn't have to endure the excruciating heartbreak.

It was clear to me that I was never meant to have any happiness in my life. My childhood and teen years had been one long string of disappointments. Then I'd ended up with this monster. With Colt, I'd finally found someone that made me feel that life was worth living. And now, because of my sordid past, he was gone.

I stumbled off the couch. Ray turned around just as I grabbed a glass from his liquor cabinet. I smacked it on the side of his desk to give it jagged edges, deadly shards just sharp enough to cut a throat. Ray stepped back. But it wasn't his throat I was heading for. I shoved the glass toward my neck. Ray's eyes widened, and he lunged for the glass. I put a gash in my shoulder as he knocked it from my hand.

He stared at me. "You had it all here. Money. An easy life."

Tears clouded my vision. "Life with you was never easy. But when you started drinking, it became unbearable."

Ray's jaw tightened. He tossed back the bourbon and slammed his glass on the desk. "We'll see just how unbearable I can be." He reached for me as there was a knock at the door. He stopped. I used the pause to step out of his reach. His silent, menacing glare stopped my retreat.

"Yes?" he called sharply.

One of the men from outside poked his head into the office. Ray had obviously hired a whole new crew for protection. I was sure it had to do with the miserable failure of his men the night I'd made a run for it. Overwhelming sadness washed over me again as I thought back to that night, the night I'd ended up in Colt's arms.

"What is it?" Ray asked.

The man stepped inside. He was armed with a large handgun, a ridiculous contrast to the expensive, crisp suit he was wearing. He looked more prepared for a business meeting than protecting a lowlife bookie from all the people who wanted him dead. "Sir, the man who gave you information is here to collect his ten thousand dollar reward."

A derisive laugh shot from Ray's mouth. "Is he? Fucking mercenary. Tell him to get the fuck off of my property. If he doesn't leave, shoot him."

The man looked shocked.

I glanced over at Ray. "God, you've really lost your fucking mind."

He ignored my barb and glared at the man who hadn't moved yet.

"Well, is there something else?"

The man shook his head. He seemed to be thinking the same thing as me. "Nope. I'll go ask him to leave the property." With that he turned and left.

Ray faced me. "Next time one of my men is within earshot, you keep that pretty mouth shut. Now, where were we?"

TWENTY-NINE
COLT

I wiped most of the blood away from my face, but every time I talked or moved, it seemed to start flowing again. With my state of mind and body, for that matter, I wasn't thinking too straight. None of us were, it seemed. We were moving purely on adrenaline and anger. There had been no plan made, just a quick ambush. We pulled up to the street. Ward's massive house peered up over the tall trees.

Slade leaned down to get a view past a long, leafy branch. "I see some men standing out on the lawn. Looks like he's got guys positioned all around the place." He pushed his face farther forward. "Wait. What the fuck is he doing there?"

"You going to let us in on your solo conversation?" Hunter asked.

"It's that asshole who's been picking up our cargo."

"Ace? Are you sure?" I asked.

Slade squinted to make sure. "Yep, that's him."

"That asshole. He was asking questions about Jade on our last drop."

Hunter looked at me in the backseat. "You never said anything."

"He had the flyer with her picture and the reward offer. He was asking me while he had his gun against my head. I told him I didn't know her, but he'd already been asking around about her and people had mentioned my name. I guess we have him to blame for the whole thing going down like this."

Hunter turned forward. "He must be at the house to collect his reward." He pulled the guns out from the glove box. Unfortunately, mine was still at the cottage. But Slade and Hunter had theirs, and I was armed with enough rage and determination that I wasn't going to need one.

Slade checked his bullets. "Been awhile since we needed to use these." There was an edge of hesitation in his voice. We'd been in plenty of fights, but a brawl always took on a whole different layer when everyone was armed. And keeping the police out of it was going to be impossible.

I leaned forward. "You guys already saved my ass once today. I would have been shark bait by now. Why don't I just go up alone? I'll take a gun and see if I can negotiate my way inside."

Slade looked back at me and laughed dryly. "Negotiate? Have you taken a look at yourself, dude? Trust me you aren't that sparkly pretty Colt that the girls all yearn for. No one is going to let you inside."

"You're not going alone," Hunter said in a tone that meant don't bother to argue. We climbed out of Slade's car and headed up the street to the house.

As we stepped into view, three of the men posted out front took off and climbed into a black Cadillac. They took off down the road and never looked back. Slade looked at Hunter. "Must have been that ugly mug of yours. They just ran off for their mommies like the boogie man was chasing them."

We stepped onto the front lawn. Ace was on the front porch. He didn't look shocked to see us. "Thought you boys might show up."

We stopped midway. "You told Ward that I was with the girl?"

"Yeah. Sorry about that. It was ten grand, and I figured you were just having fun with his girl. Didn't know there was actually something between you or that Ward was such an asshole. He stiffed me on the ten grand, so I've decided to help you out."

"How'd you get those dimwits to leave?" Slade asked.

Ace shrugged and put his gun in his holster. "Let's just say that I can drop some names that will make grown men like those douchebags shit their pants." He looked at me. "You look a little raw, but are you going in to get the girl, or what?"

"Yep." I slid past him. Hunter and Slade followed. I heard a muffled scream coming from behind a door. I kicked it and the door flew open. Ward had ripped Jade's shirt open. Her mouth was swollen and red as she tried to fight him off.

She looked up. "Colt!" she cried.

Ward jumped up from the couch. Hunter grabbed him. I dropped to my knees in front of the couch and swept Jade into my arms.

"You're alive," she said between sobs.

"Seems that way."

She tucked herself against me. "Don't ever scare me like that again."

"Funny, I was just about to say the same thing to you." I lifted her into my arms.

Hunter had Ward in a chokehold. Ward's eyes were bulging with rage and a lack of oxygen. "Just give me the word, Colt, and I'll squeeze his neck flat," Hunter said.

I shook my head. "Nope. He's mine. Take Jade out of here."

Hunter released Ward. He bent over coughing and gasping for air.

I put Jade in Hunter's arms. He carried her out but Slade stuck around. I figured he would.

Ward ran to his desk where his gun sat. I was on him before he could reach it. I turned him to face me. His nervous gaze flicked to the door. "How did you get past my men?"

"Do you mean the guys who just scooted to their car with their tails between their legs?"

His eyes went wide.

"What's the matter? You look worried."

He backed up and his desk stopped his retreat. "Get out before I call the police."

"Good idea. Then Jade can tell them what you've done to her, and I'll probably mention being kidnapped and threatened with death." I took a step toward him. "You are officially done with Jade. When I leave here, you're going to wish you'd never gone looking for her. Who the fuck am I kidding? You're going to wish you'd never met her." I grabbed hold of his shirt. "Hope you have a lot of fucking aspirin in this big ole house."

THIRTY

JADE

Hunter wanted to take me back to the car but I wouldn't let him. He gave me his sweatshirt to cover up. My head was still spinning and every bone in my body ached, but I knew everything would feel right again once Colt walked out of the house. Seeing him alive had been like waking up from a horrible nightmare.

A shiver ran through me. Hunter placed his arm around me.

"Will he be all right?" I asked. "He was such a mess." I swallowed hard. "Ray told me Colt was dead."

"Amy called right after you left. We headed to the beach house first. Good thing. They were just pulling in with the van as we were leaving."

I wrapped my arms around him. "Thank you. I'm so sorry I brought all of this down on you guys."

"Nothing to be sorry about. I'm glad you're with us. And I know Street is thrilled."

"I'm thrilled too."

Several minutes passed. "Do you think they're all right?" I asked.

"I doubt Ward is, but I'm sure Colt and Slade are fine."

Slade came out first. I ran halfway up the lawn to greet him. He pointed behind with his thumb. "Colt's coming."

I took a few steps. The front door opened and Colt walked out. He was stretching out his fingers and his red knuckles. He looked at me.

Even black and blue, he was a sight to send a girl's heart racing. My feet nearly flew out from under me as I ran to him. I threw my arms around him and broke into tears the second his arms encircled me.

I peered up at his face. "I love you."

"I love you too, *lucky number one*." He attempted a wink. "Ouch, shit that hurts."

EPILOGUE
COLT

One month later

From the front porch steps, we could see the sun sinking below the horizon. We'd been living together in the cottage for a month. After my final encounter with Ward, he'd been sufficiently convinced never to come near Jade again. She was free of the asshole for good, and we started building a life together. Jade had been working on the garden, planting roses and vegetables, while I'd gotten busy fixing all the things that needed repair. The place was really starting to look like it had when Noddy had lived there.

Jade breathed in deeply and lowered her head against my shoulder as she let out a long sigh. "The ocean breeze always brings this amazing scent with it."

I smiled. "I don't know if I'd always call it amazing. Sometimes it's pretty funky smelling."

She elbowed me. "You know what I mean. It's the fragrance of adventure, of faraway places and—"

"And fish and oil tankers," I added.

"Stop, you party pooper."

I put my arm around her. "You're right. Sorry. What has you in such a dreamy mood today?"

"Just happy. I'm sitting with my prince charming in front of his very cozy castle and, for the first time, there's nothing terrible about my life. Oh, did I tell you Jack has hired me back on? So I'll have a job, and I get to work with my best friend."

I grabbed her around the waist and lifted her onto my lap. "Excuse me, but I thought I was your best friend."

She kissed my chin. "You are too, but in a different way. In fact, you're my best everything."

"Best everything. I like that. Now, I think this prince should carry his princess into his cozy castle and strip her of all her finery so that they can fuck like two peasants."

She laughed. "Why can't we fuck like royalty?"

I lowered my mouth to hers. "Something tells me that peasants have a lot more fun in the sack than the snobby royals." I lowered my mouth to hers and we kissed.

HEART OF STONE

STONE BROTHERS BOOK 2

ABOUT THE AUTHOR

With a long list of amazing romances, *NYT* and *USA TODAY* Bestselling author Tess Oliver has the perfect read for you! Visit TessOliver.com to see all available titles.

Anna Hart is a pseudonym of Tess Oliver and her books include the steamy Stone Brothers and Silk Stocking Inn series.

Printed in Great Britain
by Amazon